FAERIEGROUND

Believe

by beth bracken & kay fraser

illustrated by odessa sawyer

capstone young readers

FAERIEGROUND IS PUBLISHED BY
CAPSTONE YOUNG READERS
A CAPSTONE IMPRINT
1710 ROE CREST DRIVE
NORTH MANKATO, MINNESOTA 56003
WWW.CAPSTONEYOUNGREADERS.COM

LIBRARY OF CONGRESS CATALOGING-IN-PUBLICATION DATA IS
AVAILABLE ON THE LIBRARY OF CONGRESS WEBSITE.
ISBN: 978-1-62370-113-0
ISBN: 978-1-62370-281-6 (EBOOK)
SUMMARY: THE KINGDOMS IN FAERIEGROUND ARE THREATENED
BY WAR, AND NO ONE CAN BE SURE WHO IS ON WHICH SIDE.
SOLI WANTS TO BELIEVE THAT HER FRIENDS WILL COME RESCUE
HER FROM THE CROWS, BUT WILL LUCY AND KHEELAN'S
ALLEGIANCE TO THE FAERIES OF ROSELAND HOLD THEM BACK?
IN THE FINAL BOOK OF THE FAERIEGROUND SERIES, READERS
WILL FIND OUT IF FRIENDSHIP, LOVE, AND TRUST CAN PREVAIL
OVER THE EVIL THAT PLAGUES THE FAERIEGROUND.

THIS BOOK IS ALSO AVAILABLE AS FOUR LIBRARY-BOUND
EDITIONS:
THE HIDDEN THINGS 978-1-4342-9185-1
THE SEVENTH KINGDOM 978-1-4342-9186-8
RETURN TO THE CROWS 978-1-4342-9187-5
PROMISE 978-1-4342-9188-2

BOOK DESIGN BY K. FRASER
ALL PHOTOS © SHUTTERSTOCK WITH THESE EXCEPTIONS:
AUTHOR PORTRAIT © K. FRASER
ILLUSTRATOR PORTRAIT © ODESSA SAWYER
PRINTED IN CHINA.
032014
008082RRDF14

"Those who don't believe in magic will never find it."
– Roald Dahl

For Etta, my daughter. — BB
To the love of my life and best friend JB — KF

Once a baby was born in the faerieground.

The baby was beautiful. She was well loved and cared for. Her mother adored her. Everyone adored her. She was treated like a princess.

But her mother couldn't stay. Her mother had to leave, as much as she loved the baby. And so the baby was raised by her father.

It would be nice to say he tried his best, but it wouldn't be true.

The baby grew into a young woman, and she hated her mother. She felt left behind and abandoned. She felt betrayed. She felt alone in the faerieground. She didn't have a friend in the world.

The faerieground is still there, just past a wish made in the woods . . .

Part 1

Lucy

"No," my mother says again.

And I run into my room and slam the door. Again.

For a month now, we've been doing this dance, my mom and I. I beg her to help me. She says no. I get mad. She stays calm. (That only makes me madder.)

For a month, I've asked her to help. For a month, I've cried and screamed and begged and made all kinds of promises and tried everything.

But she won't help me. And without her help, I don't know how I can get back to the faerieground.

If it hadn't been for the shocked look on my mom's face when I came back, I'd almost start to believe the whole thing was a dream.

I mean, it doesn't feel real, does it? It doesn't sound like something that happens to a normal thirteen-year-old girl in Mearston.

I still barely believe it, and I was there.

First, Soli wished me away, and I found myself in a faerie kingdom. My mother had always warned me to stay away from Willow Forest, but I didn't think it could actually happen. Especially not to me.

There I was, surrounded by dark, angry faeries. Tossed into a prison cell. Made to sleep on stone. Yelled at by their queen, Calandra.

I wasn't alone in the cell. First Kheelan, a faerie warrior, and then Caro—

Caro, the Betrayer.

At least I wasn't alone. And then Soli found her way to the kingdom, just as Calandra had hoped she would.

Soli, my best friend in the entire world. My only real friend.

Once I got back home, I tried to tell a few people what had happened to me. To Soli. To all of us. But everyone thought I was crazy.

Who would believe that Soli, known at our school for being a bookworm and quiet and not much else, was a faerie queen?

Half-faerie, but same difference.

Who would believe that now, she was still in the faerie realm?

Her mother had sent a note to the school. Said that their family had moved.

Their house was boarded up. Anyone could see that the whole family was gone.

Everyone knew that Soli was adopted. But no one would believe that Soli's real mother had been Queen of the faeries. And no one could possibly believe, even if I'd bothered telling this much of the story, that once Soli discovered the truth about her life and put on the Dark Crown, Calandra withered and died. Or that I would have died, too, if the evil sect of faeries known as the Crows hadn't taken me and healed me, but kept me a prisoner.

And if it hadn't been for the necklace clutched in my hand when I found myself back on my own doorstep in Mearston, I wouldn't have believed any of it myself.

But I do.

I don't know what happened, how I came back. I had dressed as if I was going for a hunt and slid through the Crows' nest. No one suspected me. No one tried to stop me.

In a room no bigger than a closet, I found the necklace. It's almost exactly like the green one my mother wore for years. The one she gave to Soli when Soli went after me into the faerieground. Only mine is blue.

I say it's mine, but it's no more mine than anyone else's. Especially since my mother took it.

I used to feel close to my mother. I thought she was one of my best friends, really. I guess I was jealous that she cared so much for Soli. But knowing now that Soli was placed in her care after being taken from the Queen— now it makes sense.

But the point is, I always trusted my mother. And especially after my dad died, it felt like me and her against the whole world. Lucy and Andria, going through life together, figuring it out.

That's all changed now.

It isn't that she doesn't believe my story. It isn't that at all. In fact, I think there's more to the story, parts of it that she knows that I have only the barest inkling of.

Because I know my mother was there, once.

I know she was in love with the leader of the Crows, probably way before he was the leader.

And I know that her sister, Soli's real mother, Queen Calandra, left Mearston and went to the faerieground to get her back.

I know that whatever my mother was doing there, it was so bad, so dangerous, so terrifying, that Calandra risked her own life in order to send my mother home.

I don't know what she was doing.

But I know what her face looked like when she saw the blue necklace dangling from my hand.

It's the same look you see on those specials on TV about drug addicts.

A look like: "I need to have that."

A look like: "I want that."

A look like: "I don't care who I have to hurt. That will be mine."

And she took it away from me and hid it.

She said she would keep it safe. I think her exact words were, "That could hurt you. I'll make sure no one can find it."

But as far as I know, no one, faerie or otherwise, could possibly know that I have it. Except for those faeries called the Ladybirds. They know everything.

Anyway, she took it away from me and wouldn't tell me where she put it. She doesn't wear it. I even crept into her room one night while she was sleeping to make sure it wasn't clasped secretly around her neck. It's gone.

And that isn't the worst of it. That wasn't the last time that my mother betrayed me.

Two nights after I came home, I woke up in the night to the sound of glass breaking.

A rock had been thrown through my bedroom window. There was a paper tied to it. The paper had words on it, written in some other language—not even a language, some code of symbols. Words, but no words I knew.

Of course, terrified, I brought it to my mother. I didn't know what it meant. Was it a threat? Had the Crows discovered that I'd taken the necklace? Were they coming to get me? Had something terrible happened to Soli?

My mother knows everything about faeries, so I thought she'd translate the words for me. I went into her room and turned on the light. She was already awake.

"What was that sound?" she asked. There was a suspicious tone to her voice, like she thought I'd broken the window myself.

"The window broke," I said. "Someone threw this through."

I showed her the paper and the rock.

She narrowed her eyes. "Do you know what it says?" she asked.

"Of course not," I said. "I thought you might. It's from the faeries, isn't it?"

She took the paper off of the rock, turned it around. "I don't know what it says," she told me. "It's probably gibberish. It's probably one of your friends playing a trick on you or something. Or a boy, some idiot's messed-up way of flirting. What about that boy, the one you told me you kissed at the basketball game? The one Soli likes?"

Jaleel, she meant. If it hadn't been for him, none of this would have happened. If I hadn't kissed him, the boy my best friend liked, Soli and I wouldn't have had a fight. She wouldn't have wished me away in the middle of Willow Forest. We never would have gone to the faerieground.

"It's not from a boy," I said. "It's got to be from the faeries."

"Forget about the faeries, Lucy," she told me.

"I can't, Mom," I said. "I have to go back. Maybe this is information I need to get back. Can you figure out any of the words? Or do you have books that could help me figure it out?"

"No. And even if I did, you're not going back there. Ever." Then she got out of bed. She went to her dresser, rummaged through a drawer, and pulled out a box of matches.

"What are you doing?" I asked.

She didn't answer. Instead, she went into the bathroom.

For a minute, I didn't understand what she was doing. Then I smelled the smoke. The burning paper.

"No!" I screamed.

And by the time I got into the bathroom, the paper was ashes.

So for a month, this has been going on. I beg her to help me go back. She says no. We barely speak, otherwise.

I go to school, and I come home through the woods, wishing the whole time.

Wishing out loud.

Wishing while singing.

Wishing while pulling the leaves off a four-leaf clover.

Wishing inside my head.

Wishing backward.

Wishing in Spanish.

I don't talk to my friends about the faeries anymore. I did that first week, but they made fun of me so much that I just laughed it off, said it was a dream I had, and after a few days they forgot.

Although sometimes they still ask if I've seen any faeries lately.

I wish I had.

2

Soli

After a month in the Crows' nest, I'm starting to forget what any other place feels like.

I barely remember my own room, my bed at home. I only know this small, soft bed in this stone-walled room.

I barely remember the food my mother made: I have little memories of it, but mostly I just taste the soup and bread they feed me here.

I barely remember my mother's voice. I only know the call of the Crows.

After I chose to stay, after I wished away Kheelan and Jonn and sent Lucy back home, for a few days I thought about nothing except escaping. I held tight to the letter Calandra wrote when she was here, fifteen or so years ago. I kept the key I found with it clutched in my hand. When no one was looking, I tried it in every keyhole I could find.

Now I have given up.

After all, what is there to escape to? The Crows would only find me again. And I'm here to save my kingdom. I can't fight against Georg, the king of the Crows. I can't do anything to stop him. And the magic that keeps the doors locked from me—even though everyone else here can go in and out—is magic I can't even begin to touch.

They have taken my crown, and with it the seal that strengthens my power.

They have taken my bravery and my voice.

I do what I'm told. I eat what I'm given. I bathe when they say I can bathe. (It's every other day, it seems like.) I'm not locked in my room, but I can't exactly walk freely around the castle.

They aren't cruel to me, but they aren't kind. They don't chain my wrists, they don't hurt me, they don't starve me, but they don't care about me and I know it.

They don't treat me like a queen.

And sometimes I wonder if I even was one to begin with.

The one thing I do that's still what a queen would do: I haven't angered them. It's all I can do to protect the people I love, the people who live in the kingdom that should be mine. I don't want to make the Crows mad enough that they threaten my kingdom. I don't want anyone there to be hurt.

Especially Kheelan.

I think about Kheelan all the time.

How many days were we together, really? Four? I can't even count them. Somehow they were as good as a lifetime. As if we'd been together forever and always would be.

When I'm alone, at night, in my dark room, all I can think of are his eyes. The gentle way he kissed me. How he believed in me.

If he could see me now, a prisoner. Hardly the Queen of Roseland, like I'm supposed to be.

Or maybe I'm not supposed to be at all.

I have given up. I expect to die here, and probably not for a very long time.

But I do keep track of days. I scratch one little line

into the headboard of my bed, one for each morning that I wake up and this still isn't a dream, still is my life.

Thirty-one days since my first night here alone, Caro knocks at my door and then comes in before I can answer.

"Dinner," she says, but she's not carrying a tray. "Now."

I frown, confused.

"And you'll have to put on something nicer," she says. She goes to my small wardrobe, rummages around. "Nothing here will work. I'll be back."

I wait.

A minute later, she comes back, throws a dress at me. It's a simple white dress, but the fabric is far softer than silk—something I've never touched before.

"What is this made of?" I ask.

She shrugs. "Dandelion, I think," she says. "Now put it on."

I wait for her to leave, but she doesn't go.

"Could you—could you give me privacy?" I ask, and she rolls her eyes, but steps outside.

I take off my clothes—a pair of worn pants, a long-sleeved T-shirt, things that belonged to Calandra, once—and slide the dress on. It fits perfectly, and it smells like Caro.

She knocks on the door again, impatient. "Hurry up," she says. "My father is waiting."

And I follow her out the door.

She leads me—glancing behind her every so often, to make sure I haven't run away, I guess—to a dining room. I've eaten all of my meals so far in my room. Usually Caro delivers them, or one of the guards.

Today, though, it seems I am eating with Caro and her father, who waits for us at the head of the long wood table.

"Sorry we're late," she says, swishing into her seat.

Georg nods at me and motions to the empty seat across from Caro.

"Sit, Soledad," he says.

So I do.

A servant brings out a silver platter full of food. There's a tureen of the soup I recognize. There's some kind of rich, dark meat—maybe rabbit. There's a loaf of hearty bread and a thick chunk of sweet butter. Roasted vegetables, stewed apples, carafes of juices.

At first, I don't know what to do.

It's more food than I've seen in a month, and I realize that though they haven't been starving me, they haven't been feeding me, either. I have had the same thing every day.

Toast for breakfast, with butter and wildflower honey.

Soup and bread for lunch and dinner.

Once in a while, a slice of cheese.

I look at Georg. He looks back. "Please, help yourself," he says. So I do.

We eat without talking. We eat until we are full, and then the servant brings out slices of white cake, each topped with a tiny blue flower, its petals dipped in sugar. And tea. There is tea at every meal here, it seems.

I wonder if this is how they eat every night, or if it's a special occasion. And then I feel stupid for wondering. Why would I be invited to a special event?

Georg wipes his face with a linen napkin. He looks at me again, like he's waiting for something.

"Thank you for dinner," I say. "Everything was delicious."

Caro rolls her eyes. "This wasn't anything special," she says. "We eat like this all the time."

Georg frowns at her. "Enough, Caro," he says. "Soledad is our guest tonight."

"Well, maybe she shouldn't be," she mutters, and I feel a blush creep across my face.

"Enough!" he says again, louder. His voice echoes across the room.

I pick up my tea and sip it to fill the silence.

Georg turns to Caro. "Your archery teacher told me you skipped your lesson today."

Caro sighs. "I didn't skip it, Father. I was just—I was just late."

"Why were you late?" her father asks.

"I was just late. I lost track of time. I didn't do it on purpose. And it was only a few minutes." Now a blush has spread across Caro's face.

She's hiding something.

But what?

"That's no way for a princess to behave," Georg says, shaking his head. "A princess is not late. Your mother never would have—"

"My *mother* isn't here," Caro says. "I've had to figure some things out for myself."

And she stares across the table at me until I blush again and look away.

The servants clear the plates away, and Caro leaves me alone with Georg.

"Thank you again," I say. "It's nice to eat such delicious food at a real table." Then I worry that I've sounded sarcastic, or rude, and I add, "Not that my normal meals aren't delicious."

Georg sighs. "You'll soon become used to our ways," he says. "And we'll soon become used to you." Then he stands. "Do you know the way back to your room, or shall I send for someone to help you find it?" he asks.

I smile. "I know the way, thank you," I say, and he bows slightly and opens the door for me.

Then I go one way and he goes the other.

Soli

This is the first time I've been alone in the palace. I'm tempted to explore, to learn more about the nest I'm in, but nervous—I'm sure someone must be watching me. So I go back to my room.

But when I open the door, the first thing I see is an envelope on my pillow.

The words are written in faerie, but somehow, now, I can read them.

Sweet—

I don't know if this letter will make it to you. I'm taking a risk in sending it, I know that. I can't be sure I'm doing the right thing, but I can't stand to think of you all alone.

I know you won't be able to respond. That's much riskier. But I'll keep writing until I see you again.

And I'll be careful what I say just in case it falls into the wrong hands—or talons.

I can't tell you how I'm getting this letter to you. As I said, I can't be sure it'll even arrive.

But I should start with the other important things that I need to make sure you know.

I know you're wondering, so I'll be sure to tell you: your people are safe.

My father and I are safe, and I hope you are, too. We were suddenly home, so the journey wasn't hard.

(That's a joke.)

I know that your other half, too, is home; we've sent her a message.

We wait for her to cross over. I check the woods every dusk and dawn, but so far, I haven't seen her.

But at the same time, we can't just sit here forever, and so my father and I have started to plan our next step.

Your people know and trust my father, so he leads them until you return.

I can't tell you much more than that without risking ruining our plan.

What I can tell you is that I love you. I knew it right away when I saw you, and it grew stronger every time we talked or touched.

I love you now, even though we're apart.

I think of you all the time. Hoping that you're safe. Hoping that you're not sad or afraid.

You are brave, so I know you're staying strong. I just wish we could be together. And I wish I understood what happened that day, when I'd been in the Crow palace but suddenly I looked up and was home.

For some reason I think you did it, which sometimes makes me angry—why didn't you let me stay with you?—but I trust that you know what you're doing.

I don't have much more time—my messenger waits and I can't risk being late.

I'll send this now with all of my love—

yours—

K.

3

Lucy

It seems like my mom hardly ever sleeps anymore.

Every night, I wait for her to go to bed, so I can search the house for my necklace. And every night, just as I step outside my room, her door flies open.

She pretends to be sweet about it. "You need your rest, darling!" she'll say. But there's always this strange hunger in her eyes.

So I finally decide that nighttime isn't when I'll find my necklace.

And for the first time in my life, I skip school.

I get up and dress and eat breakfast as usual, toss my bags into my backpack, kiss my mother goodbye. But instead of going through the woods, I just wait there for a while.

Not for the first time, it occurs to me that I could try to find my way back by wishing in the woods. After all, that's what sent me to the faerieground the first time.

So while I wait, I try it. I find the spot where I was when Soli wished me away, and I wish. I wish. I cross my fingers and wish. I wish on a four-leaf clover. I wish on the stars I can't see because it's daytime. I wish on the tips of trees. I pretend to blow out birthday candles and wish on that.

My wish is always the same: "I wish I was back in the faerieground."

Nothing works.

Maybe it only worked for Soli that time because she was a faerie. Or half-faerie, anyway.

After I've waited for an hour, I pick up my backpack and head back home.

I go in through the back gate. And as I'm almost to the back door, I trip on a clump of dirt.

When my dad was alive, he spent a lot of time in our yard. He didn't just mow the lawn like other dads do. He also grew fruit trees and planted huge vegetable gardens and the most beautiful flowerbeds.

After he died, they all turned to weeds. Except for the fruit trees, but I swear the apples and pears don't taste as sweet as they did when he was alive.

So our yard and gardens are a mess, but this clump of dirt is different, somehow. It looks fresh—there's still green grass on one side. And it doesn't look like an animal dug it up. It looks like a human did. With a shovel.

When I bend down and pull it away from the ground, the dirt looks loose. Like someone just dug something up here and piled the dirt back in the hole.

And when I brush some dirt away, a corner of a metal box glints up at me.

Inside the box is a pile of blue mushrooms. An orange peel. A shard from a broken mirror. Two pieces of white lace. A clump of dried lavender.

My missing necklace.

And a crumpled business card.

It just says *Molly Murry, Mearston Historical Society,* and there's a phone number.

I slip on the necklace and head into town.

Soli

The letter must be from Kheelan.

Right?

Who else would write, and call me "Sweet," and sign it "K"?

But how did he get it to me?

The envelope was open.

Who read it before I did?

Is it a trick? Something Caro's doing to make me mad? Something one of the other Crows is doing?

Is that why they asked me to dinner, so that while I was gone, someone could sneak into my room and leave the letter on my bed?

All I have now are more questions. And a smudged, crumpled paper shoved between my mattress and the sheets.

Kheelan, thinking of me.
Or a cruel joke meant to hurt me.
Those are the only options.

I want it to be the first thing, but it seems more likely to be the second.

I lie awake late. There are no clocks here, but it must be nearly dawn, and I can't sleep. My body thrums with nervous energy.

If there was one letter, will there be another?

Will he risk sending more?

And what are his and his father's plans?

A true queen, I think, would know what to do. A true queen wouldn't lie in her bed, away from her people, and cry out of loneliness.

And fear.

A true queen wouldn't be afraid.

That's something that makes me think the letter can't be real. The K who wrote the letter sent it to someone who was brave, and that person isn't me.

But I suppose real bravery isn't not feeling afraid. It's being afraid and doing it anyway.

Like when I came into the faerieground to find Lucy.

Or when I fought against Georg to save my friends.

Or when I chose to stay here, all alone.

Not that I had much of a choice about any of that. But I did it. I was afraid and I did it anyway.

Outside my little window, the sun begins to rise. I can mark another day here.

And this time, I have a glimmer of hope. A piece of paper that might have been touched by the boy I love. He might have written to me because he truly misses me. He loves me.

Or maybe not.

A soft knock comes at my door. It's Caro, with my breakfast.

"You're awake?" she says. Normally I'm asleep now, and wake up only to find my breakfast tray waiting.

"I couldn't sleep," I say. I can't tell her why, of course.

"What are you going to do all day?" she asks, a look of real curiosity on her face.

I shrug, look around the room. "Nap, I guess," I say. I nap most days.

What else is there to do?

"I have a lot of books in my room," she offers. "If you get bored and want something to do besides nap."

"What kind of books?" I ask.

She tosses her head. "All kinds," she tells me. "Some are even from the other side."

"Like, human books?"

"Yeah, I guess. From other people who have crossed over and left them here. Funny how you people seem to leave books wherever you go."

I think of the time my family went on vacation and stayed in a cabin right next to a lake. There were dusty paperbacks in the cabin's main room. One of them was in Swedish, but I read the others: mysteries, mostly.

"Thank you," I say. "I'd love to read a book."

"You know where my room is, right?" she says. "I have to get ready for my—for a lesson. But you can go and get one when you're done with breakfast."

"Why are you being so nice to me?" I ask.

She shrugs, and a smile flits across her face. "I don't know," she says. "I guess I decided I should get used to having you around, since you're probably going to be here forever."

Then she turns on her heel and is gone.

I do go to her room after breakfast, and I find the shelf of books. Some of them are just like the ones I remember from Lake Kabetogama.

Boring cowboy stories. Books with women in tight dresses on the cover.

But they aren't all like that.

After I look past all the worn paperbacks, I notice a few hardcovers, bound in what looks like leather but feels like silk. The spines don't have titles, but when I pull each book off the shelf, the covers have words in faerie.

The Coming of the Crows

Crossing Between Lands

Human Myths

The Golden Age of Faeries

Complete Encyclopedia of Human-World Flora

A History of Roseland

A Guide to Spells

Prophecy of the Ladybirds, 4th Edition

I pull *A History of Roseland* off the shelf, and it falls open.

An envelope is tucked between the pages.

Sweet—

I'm writing this letter two weeks after the first. I thought I should tell you that because I'm not sure when you will have received the first. If it made it at all.

I hope very much that I can trust the person helping me reach you with these notes, but it's a risk.

It's all a risk.

It will be worth all the risk when I see your face again.

Remember that time you asked me if we'd ever be real?

I knew what you meant: would we grow old together, or even grow at all together.

Or was it just because I was charmed by your importance. Or was it just because war brings people together.

(And this is a war. Right now the battle is just brewing, but it IS a war.)

I told you then that we would be. And I meant it.

I still mean it.

I don't know how it is in the world you grew up in. But here, it's easy to spot a soulmate. Something about the eyes. Faeries just have ways to understand each other, to know when we've met the one we belong with.

That doesn't mean that all love affairs last forever, but when we see the person we're right for now, we know.

I think you know, too, even if only half your blood is faerie.

I hope, hope, hope you feel the same way I do.

And I think, too, that in your world we would be too young for real love, but here, our hearts know the right time.

But that's only part of why I'm writing.

I still wait in the woods at dusk and dawn, but no sign yet of your other half.

We have sent out missives to five of our sister kingdoms. (There are seven, including the Crows and Roseland.) The Crows will have learned of this already, or maybe are learning of it as you read this letter. They have eyes everywhere, after all.

I'll include a copy of the letter so that you know what it says. If this is how the Crows find out (which I doubt) then so be it.

I hope to have better news for you soon and to be with you.

We will be fighting for you—

yours—

K.

Inside the envelope there's a small piece of parchment.

Roseland Calls

Our queen, Soledad, is held by the Crows.

We ask for your help.

Night of the first new moon
Roseland Palace

Now I believe that the letters are from Kheelan.

And I believe that they're going to fight to get me back.

I sigh. Doesn't he get it?

I don't want to be rescued.

This is the way I'm keeping Roseland safe.

But what I don't understand is how the letters are coming to the Crows. And how this one ended up in a book in Caro's room.

Just as I think that, she sweeps in, and I barely have enough time to hide the envelope in my pocket.

"Finding anything to read? she asks.

I show her the cover of *A History of Roseland*. She rolls

her eyes. "I had to read that a few years ago," she tells me. "Pretty boring. Your people haven't even had that many interesting wars or anything."

"What about your people?" I ask, letting the book fall open. I glance down and notice that the text is tiny.

I can't believe Caro had to read it a few years ago. She's my age. This looks like a book someone would read in college.

"My people love war," she says. "That's how we've gotten where we are today."

"And where is that?" I ask.

She shrugs, looks around the room. "Here, I guess," she says. "With the Queen of Roseland trapped in our nest, we'll soon rule all of faerieland."

But there's sadness in her voice that I didn't expect.

4

Lucy

The Mearston Historical Society is a small white building on the edge of town. It's old, probably almost as old as Mearston itself. It used to be the town hall, a long time ago. That's what the sign outside says, anyway. And then the new town hall was built in 1953.

I've never been inside. It's always just seemed like the kind of boring building that kids don't go to.

And when I do walk in, I see that I was right. My feet make the old floorboards squeak, and a little bell rings as the door closes behind me. I start to look around. I'm in a quiet room that smells a little bit like sawdust and paint. There are a few displays of old pictures and letters, and those seem kind of interesting, but not really. There's a slice of a huge old tree cut down in Willow Forest in 1987, and that's sort of cool: it has more than a hundred rings and is really wide.

Then I spot the bookshelf. The books on it are really old. Maybe one of them will have some kind of mention of the faeries. After all, Mearston has been here for a long time, and I know that my mother and her sister can't have been the first ones to cross over into the faerieground.

I bend down to look at the shelf. But before I can read any of the books' titles, someone coughs, and I jump.

A woman is sitting at an old wooden desk at the back of the room. I didn't see her when I walked in—it's almost like she just appeared there.

"Can I help you?" she asks, standing up. She looks like she's about the same age as my mom, but she's much rounder and shorter, and her hair has started to turn gray around her temples. She walks toward me, and I can see that she's wearing a nametag: Molly Murry.

"Um, probably not," I say. "I'm looking for—"

But she gasps. "Your necklace," she says. "Where did you get that?"

I look down. The blue pendant, which I'd thought I'd tucked away inside my shirt, is gleaming on my chest.

"Um, it's nothing special," I say, dropping it inside my shirt. "Just thought it was pretty."

"It certainly is," she says, and her eyes flash.

"So anyway," I say, trying to change the subject. "I have to write a paper for school, and the librarian suggested I come in here for some information. So maybe I'll just look around a little bit? I don't want to get in your way."

"No trouble at all, dear," the woman says. Then her eyes narrow. "Aren't you Andria's daughter?"

"Yes, I am," I say, suddenly nervous. "Are you a friend of hers? I don't remember ever meeting you before."

"Oh, she and I haven't seen each other in a while," Molly Murry says. "We were in school together. I was in Calandra's—"

She stops, and I try to keep my face still and calm. "I was a friend of a friend of hers," she says finally.

"Oh. Cool!" I say. "I'll tell her you said hello, Ms. Murry."

"Please do," she says. "Now. What's your paper on? I'm sure I can help."

I take a deep breath. If this woman knew Calandra, and knew what happened to her, maybe she actually knows a little about the faeries.

But I have to be careful.

"It's on faeries," I say slowly. "You know, the, like, magical kind?"

She gazes at me. "Go on," she says.

"I don't know," I say, pretending I'm way dumber than I really am. "A couple of the girls at school say they've seen these, like, mystical people in the forest? Like, you know, with wings and magic wands and all that fancy stuff. And when I was little, my mom always told me these faerie stories. I know it's all totally made up, but I have to write about a mythical belief for my composition class, and I thought I could maybe find out what other people here have thought, like, a long time ago. And then write about that."

Molly Murry relaxes, now that she can see that I'm just a dumb teenager, not someone trying to get real information.

But she keeps glancing toward the thin chain around my neck.

"I'm sure I can help," she says. "In fact, there's a long history of belief of faeries here in Mearston."

"Oh, cool!" I say. "Is there, like, a website I can go to or something?"

She smiles. "Mostly books," she says. "I don't know of any website in particular that would help you, although I'm sure you could do a Google search and find many interesting stories."

"Okay," I say. "Well, I guess I'll look at the books, then."

She turns to the bookshelf. And as she's bent over, plucking some books off the shelf, she whispers, "You can't fool me, Lucy."

I sigh. "Okay," I say. "I'm sorry."

"I know what your mother has done. Why don't you just ask her?"

"Because she won't tell me," I mutter.

Molly Murry straightens up. "How much do you know already?"

"Enough," I say. Then I take a deep breath. "I need to get there. It's kind of an emergency."

She studies my face. "You have the way," she says. "You have the map, anyway. It won't get you across, but only a faerie can."

"What do you mean? What map?" I ask, confused.

"The pendant," she whispers.

I lift it out of my shirt, and she takes it in her hand, turning it over.

"See how it's translucent?" she asks. "You look through it to see the trails the faeries have left. I can't imagine how you got this, though. It's been lost—"

The bell tinkles at the front door, and she pulls away. I quickly hide the necklace under my clothes.

"Hello!" she trills at the old woman who's just walked in. "I'll be with you in a moment, Mrs. O'Leary. I've found out a little more information about the history of your store."

Then Molly Murry turns back to me. "Have you been there?" I ask.

"No," she says, and an odd look flashes across her face again. "No, I never have."

Soli

Caro says I can go into her room whenever she's at her lessons and borrow books, so I read everything. All of them, even the ones that are as thick as college textbooks.

I have nothing else to do, after all.

I learn a lot. So much about my people. The history of faeries, it turns out, is just as long as the history of humans, and more of it is written down. I learn about my father's side of my family tree—the wars they won, the land they ruled. It's all so amazing and strange.

It turns out that thousands of years ago, when the faeries began recording their history, all of faerieland was one kingdom. It's much bigger than Willow Forest, which I kind of guessed at already. After all, how could so much fit inside the woods outside my town?

The kingdom was happy for a thousand years, but then a bad king took the throne.

No one knows why he did what he did, but he split the kingdom into seven and assigned six other kings and queens to rule them. Families were torn apart, and after that, there were wars.

One of the kingdoms became Roseland. One queen ruled over a kingdom of all women who became the Ladybirds.

There was a kingdom called Equinox, and one called Waterwind, and one called River, one called Westwood, and one called Eastwood.

The one called Equinox become the Crows.

After a few days of reading and trying to remember everything, I start to feel overwhelmed. Caro finds me in her room after her lesson, surrounded by books.

"What are you doing?" she asks.

"Trying to remember it all," I say.

She rolls her eyes, crosses to her wardrobe, and pulls out another book. "Here," she says, thrusting it at me. "Take this."

I open it. It's just blank pages. I look back at her, and she tosses me a heavy gold pen.

"I'll find you a bottle of ink," she says.

I'm afraid to write anything down. "Won't they think I'm trying to plan something?" I say.

"No," she tells me. "You can't get out of here, Soli. And all the Crows know that."

She laughs, one of her trademark cruel laughs. "You're just a girl, and they know it."

But now, surrounded by the startling history of my family, I'm starting to realize I'm more than just a girl.

Soli

The next letter is slipped under my door in the middle of the night.

Sweet—

I've checked the woods at dawn and dusk each day for your other half. No sign of her. Perhaps she doesn't want to be found.

I'll check again tonight for the last time. Tomorrow is the new moon, and the kingdoms will arrive.

It has been suggested to me that maybe you don't want us to find you.

That you didn't want to be queen, and that you'd rather be left alone.

I don't believe that.

But either way, tomorrow we form our plan, and soon we will come for you.

I hope you'll be ready, and I hope you'll be happy.

yours——

K.

4

Lucy

Maybe the faeries don't want me to come back.

That's all I can think as I run through the woods, looking ridiculous with the necklace in front of my right eye.

Maybe they sent me away on purpose. Maybe Soli doesn't want me to come back either.

But that won't stop me now.

Molly Murry was right. The pendant is like a map. Or a magnifying glass, maybe. When I hold it in front of my eye, the woods look different, and there are glowing trails

leading through the woods. It isn't hard, once I get going, to find the right one. It's the one that feels right. Maybe that's another power the necklace has.

The glowing path leads me to an old willow tree, and when I get close, a figure steps out from behind the tree.

"Kheelan!" I cry, stopping in my tracks.

"Lucy," he says, smiling. "Finally."

He hugs me, but I pull back. "What do you mean, finally?" I ask.

"I thought you didn't want to be found. I've been here twice a day since we were sent away from the Crows' nest. I've come at dusk and dawn, waiting for you."

"Dusk and dawn? Why would I be in the woods then?" I ask, smiling.

He smiles back. "I don't know. I just thought—"

And we laugh.

"I thought you didn't want to find me!" I say. "I was sure no one wanted me. I've been trying to figure out how to get to the faerieground myself, to be honest. I have this—"

I show him the pendant, and he smiles. "The blue

one," he says. "The Equinox pendant." When he sees my confused face, he shakes his head. "I'll explain later," he says. "But there are many people who'll be glad you have that."

"Can you bring me back?" I ask.

He nods. "Of course. That's why I'm here. In fact, tonight was the last time I planned to come. It's the last chance. Tomorrow—" He stops. "What was that?"

I look around. "I didn't hear anything."

"Someone is here," he whispers. "We need to hurry. Are you ready? Do you have what you need?"

"Let's go," I say. "I don't need anything."

He takes my hand and pulls me into the faerieground.

Part 2

5

Soli

I lie back in bed.

And I count the cracks in the plaster ceiling again, trying to pass the time, trying to get through the days. Thirty-two of them today, same as yesterday. Same as every day.

I turn onto my stomach, and as I arrange the pillow under my head, something crackles beneath it.

Kheelan's letter.

For the hundredth time, I read it.

Then I shove it back under the pillow and flip around onto my back. I imagine his hand on my cheek. His tender smile, his lips on mine.

I stare at the walls surrounding me, memorizing the tenderness of his words and gestures. He called me sweet. I can picture him saying it. Something inside my chest twists.

He wants to rescue me. They all do. Even people I've never met, from five other kingdoms.

Not Lucy, though.

I think she's making the right choice. Staying home, where she belongs. Where she's safe.

She knows there is no chance here, or at least I think she must. She knows there is no hope for me.

The quest to rescue the captured Queen of Roseland is suicide, a far-fetched fairy tale. There is no way out of this place. Everyone knows that.

They can't save me.

I'm a Crow in the making. I know it. I can feel it. Not a queen. Not Roseland's queen, anyway.

I'm not the same girl that walked through these doors a month ago. If Kheelan knew, I don't know if he'd bother writing. I'm not Kheelan's sweet, Lucy's best friend, or Queen Calandra's daughter. If I ever really was any of those things.

"I'm a Crow," I whisper, testing the thought.

A knock on my door brings me back to my room.

"Done moping? Ready to do some real work?" Caro asks, walking in. She's wearing boy clothes, and her sun-colored hair is up in a high ponytail.

"Anything to get out of this room," I say, standing up.

"Father thinks you'll turn lazy if you don't get exercise," she says, "so I convinced him to let you attend my classes."

I'm surprised by the light that glows inside me at the thought. "That is very kind of you," I say, and I mean it.

I can't read her expression, but she seems relieved I'm willing to join her. "Don't thank me yet," she says, grinning. "I don't think you know what you're getting yourself into." She rummages through my drawers without asking and pulls out a pair of pants and a long-sleeved T-shirt.

I can't help but think that the clothes used to belong to my mother. I know she stayed in this room.

"Class will be tough in a dress," Caro says. "Put these on. And some boots."

"I don't have any boots," I say, looking around my tiny room, and she rolls her eyes.

"Back in a minute," she says. "I'll get you some of mine."

I dress quickly while she's gone. Caro doesn't care about privacy, so I know she won't knock when she comes back. I'm just buttoning the pants when she throws my door open.

"Here," she says, tossing a pair of boots into my room. "Hurry up. Class starts in five minutes. In the archery field behind the castle. If you're not on time, don't bother coming."

She slams the door behind her. I lace up the soft leather boots.

"I'm a Crow now," I say to the door that keeps me prisoner.

The handle has never moved for me before.

I reach out and try it.

I hear a click. The heavy door opens.

Lucy

Kheelan is like a wild creature in the woods.

His wings seem to suspend him in the air when he takes long strides. It's pretty amazing to watch him. I try not to stare as we head through the forest, but that gets harder and harder the farther we go.

It's harder to move quickly, too. I'm exhausted. We haven't even spoken since we crossed over to the faerieground—he just said, "Hurry," and I tried to.

"Come on, Lucy, keep up," Kheelan urges me.

"I'm not a faerie, you know. I'm a human girl," I call ahead to him.

He forgot I'm not Soli. He forgot I'm not one of them. He forgot I'm an average teenage girl.

"I'm sorry," he says, coming to a sudden stop. "I'm used to—"

"Soli," I say, finishing his sentence. "I know."

He nods, and his eyes become sad with the thought of her. I've never seen a boy so into a girl before. It seems real to him, as real and necessary as air.

"Is she all right?" I ask. "Where is she?" I still don't know what happened, how I was sent home.

He kicks the dirt, and twigs lift from the ground. "Nothing has been all right."

Then he tells me. How the Crow king, Caro's father, asked Soli to choose between her true love and her best friend. And how, instead, she sent us both away.

"So that's why she didn't come get me," I say.

He nods. "Have you spoken to her?" I ask.

"No," he says, his face sad. "I've sent her letters. I have someone there who helps me."

"Who?" I ask, thinking of the Crow palace and the people I met there. I didn't meet anyone who didn't seem cruel. I certainly didn't meet anyone who would help Kheelan.

"I can't say," he says. "But I think the letters are getting there safely. Although I can't be sure. She hasn't written back. She's still with the Crows, as far as I know, but—maybe she doesn't think it's safe to write."

I feel like crying when I think of the Crows. Chills run down my spine with each thought of black-feathered wings.

I don't feel brave enough to go back there.

Not yet.

"How do we get her out?" I ask.

Kheelan looks at me, and the beginnings of a smile start to spread across his face. "I'm working on it," he says. "Good thing you got here in time."

He is quiet for the rest of the walk, and I don't try to make conversation. I'm too busy thinking about my friend—my best friend, my almost-sister—trapped in the Crows' nest. I can only imagine Kheelan's frustration.

Soli is not only the leader of Roseland, but she's also his true love.

It must be really hard for him, knowing she's out there with the Crows.

After a while, he stops. "This way," he says, pushing aside a thatch of vines hiding a road.

The road to the palace is full of faeries. It is a colorful procession of soldiers bearing bright flags and banners.

And bows and arrows.

As we get closer, there begin to be tents scattered around the road. Six colors of tents, some clustered by color, some mixed together. The faerieground has always been beautiful, but it's never been so colorful. Even the flowers seem to have bloomed while I've been gone.

The gloom that overcame this palace in the past is gone, destroyed.

"I wish Soli could see this," I say.

Kheelan nods. "Me too," he says. Then he grabs my hand and squeezes it. "I think she will. Soon."

I don't say anything in return.

I'm not sure he knows how powerful the Crows are.

"What are all these people doing here?" I ask, trying to understand.

"They are here for her," Kheelan says. "For the Queen of Roseland."

"Soli?" I ask.

He nods, solemn. "It's time for us to fight the Crows for her freedom."

"Fight as in, like, weapons?" I ask.

Kheelan nods. "Fight as in war."

Soli

I hold the bow.

My right hand brushes my cheek, my left focuses on the target.

Exhale, release.

My arrow flies true to the target for the third time in a row. Not quite a bull's-eye, but close enough. I can't help but grin.

"Good work, Soledad," the trainer says. "You're a natural."

Next to me, Caro snorts. She lifts her bow, aims, releases. Her arrow hits the bull's-eye for the third time.

"You're good, but not that good," she mutters as the trainer walks away.

But I don't mind. Because of Caro, because she talked King Georg into letting me join her in classes, I've been out of my room for hours every day.

Archery. Hand-to-Hand Combat. Etiquette. History. Faerie Dialects. Flora of the Human World. Botany.

I liked school, back in Mearston, but I never liked it this much.

I'm nothing but thankful to Caro these days.

And lately I think I make a better Crow than I ever did a queen, or a daughter, or a friend, or a girlfriend.

I'm good at this.

It feels good.

I keep my stance, readying the arrow one last time. I close my eyes, letting my body take over without thinking. My right hand brushes my cheek, and then I open my eyes, see the target, release.

My arrow slices through the air and breaks Caro's in half.

Someone claps. It startles both of us, and we whirl around.

Georg stands there.

"Bravo, Soledad!" he says. "Caro, you could learn a thing or two about poise from this one. I have no doubt that had it been a man instead of a target, Soledad would have made the shot just as easily."

Caro throws her bow to the ground. "I would've killed faster than she ever could," she mutters, and then she walks away.

I look at King Georg, who laughs as his daughter storms back toward the castle.

"You should not judge her so harshly," I say before I can stop myself.

The king raises his eyebrows, and Caro stops in her tracks.

"She is the sharpest archer I've seen in this castle," I say. "She has taught me everything I know. Anything I do right is because she has taught me right."

I look down at my feet, trying to hide from the anger that I know will come. But after a moment, it's still silent, so I raise my eyes to Georg's.

He nods. "Then I suppose congratulations are due to you both," he says. He bends his head in my direction and then walks away, brushing past his daughter.

Caro smiles at me.

Lucy

Inside the faerie palace, the throne room—once dusty and dirty and full of broken windows and cobwebs—looks nothing like I remember it. The heavy draperies have been brushed back, letting light in, and the windows don't show a single crack. The room has been swept clean, and fresh-cut flowers line the surfaces.

Kheelan brought me here. He and his father, Jonn, want to talk to me. I guess it must be about the war they're planning.

At the opposite wall, a long table has been set, with chairs surrounding it. Jonn takes the head of the table. He unsheathes his sword and places it flat on the wooden surface. His son sits to his right, so I take the chair to his left. There are five more chairs at the table.

"We are ready," Jonn says. A guard throws open the heavy double doors.

"What's happening?" I whisper. But Kheelan and Jonn don't answer. They just stare, waiting, at the doors.

Then they come. Faeries march into the room. There are ten of them, walking in pairs.

The only one I recognize is Motherbird. One faerie in each pair wears a different color necklace. The necklaces all look just like Soli's, and like the one hiding under my clothes.

But these are different colors.

The necklace-wearing faeries sit down at the table, and the others—guards, I guess—stand against the wall. Motherbird sits beside me and reaches over to squeeze my hand.

Jonn clears his throat and stands. "Good morning,

my friends," he says. His deep voice echoes in the large throne room. "And thank you for coming to Roseland on such short notice."

He looks around the table, and so do I. Besides Motherbird, who wears a red necklace, there is an older man with a yellow one; a woman who looks like she's my mom's age, wearing a violet one; a white-haired woman with an orange one; and a younger man whose necklace is indigo.

"Of course you will notice that two of the Seven are not here," Jonn goes on. "We sent a messenger to Georg, but heard no response."

"Did the messenger return?" mutters the older man with the yellow necklace.

Jonn shakes his head. "No, Lotham, he didn't."

A murmur goes around the table.

"And Queen Soledad, too, is gone," Motherbird says calmly.

"Yes," Jonn says. "As you all know, Queen Soledad has been a hostage of the Crows for a month now."

I sneak a glance at Kheelan, but his face is blank.

"Now is the time," Jonn says. He looks around the table, staring at each faerie in turn.

Motherbird shifts next to me. "Now is the time," she says. But there's sadness in her voice, not fire, like in Jonn's.

I look at the other faeries. They stare at Jonn, not answering.

"The Crow kingdom has terrorized each of our own kingdoms for centuries," Jonn goes on.

"Calandra was the terrorist here," the white-haired woman says. "She almost ruined Roseland."

Jonn's nostrils flare. "Calandra—Queen Calandra— is not the point of discussion today," he says. "We have tried to deal with the Crows peacefully, but now, with Soledad—"

"Queen Soledad," Motherbird interrupts.

"Queen Soledad," Jonn says, nodding. "With Queen Soledad being held captive, we must take action."

"Who says she's captive?" asks the man wearing the indigo necklace. "What if she's choosing to stay? Who's to say—"

"She hasn't chosen that," Kheelan suddenly says.

His face is flushed with anger. Everyone turns to look at him.

"Pardon my son," Jonn says, shooting Kheelan a look. "He and Soledad have a—well, they have a special relationship. And we were with Queen Soledad at the Crow palace when it happened."

"What happened, exactly?" the white-haired woman asks. But she doesn't ask Jonn. She's looking at Motherbird.

Motherbird smiles and closes her eyes. "It seems Soledad was given a choice," she says. "She was told that she must choose between the boy, Kheelan, or her friend, Lucy. Georg wanted to make her vulnerable, so he told her to choose who would die."

"Wait a moment. Who is Lucy?" the white-haired woman asks.

Motherbird opens her eyes. She reaches over and takes my hand. "This is Lucy," she says.

"So who did she choose?" asks the older man, Lotham.

"Soledad chose herself," Motherbird says. "She used what little power she could pull away from Georg, and with it, she sent Kheelan here, and she sent Lucy home to Mearston."

"Oh," the white-haired woman says. "Lucy is human." She wrinkles her nose at me.

"Indeed she is, Calla, and there's more to her than meets the eye," Motherbird says.

"But the point is, Soli didn't choose to stay there because she wanted to be there," Kheelan says. "Right, Motherbird?"

Motherbird nods. "That's right," she says. "She was asked to choose a person who would die by the hand of the Crows, and she chose herself."

A terror runs through me.

"She's still alive, isn't she?" I whisper, and Motherbird squeezes my hand.

"Yes. She's still alive."

"War is not the answer," Lotham says. "War has never been the answer. War is what got us into this mess."

"Yes," says the younger man. "I understand that your queen is in need of rescue, but there must be some other way—"

"There is no other way, and there is no other time," says the other woman.

"Helenea, how is it possible that you can know—" Lotham starts, but Helenea holds up her hand, and he's silent.

"For far too long the kingdom has been torn apart," she says, and I know from the way she says it that she doesn't mean Roseland, or her own kingdom. "For far too long, the Seven have been separate, and now is the time, and I know we all feel that."

The faeries look at each other. They all wear blank expressions.

The younger man shakes his head.

"Montan, what is your trouble with this?" Helenea asks.

"I do not like the idea of unity," Montan says. "My kingdom lives in peace, far away from the Crows."

"But your brothers and sisters do not," Motherbird says, looking at him directly. "And if the Crows take us, they will soon take you."

Silence takes over the throne room.

"The unity of our kingdoms is our strength," Jonn says. "The numbers are in our favor. We can rescue the Queen and save us all if we are united."

"Let's vote," says Calla, and the other faeries nod.

"It is clear that I—and all of Roseland—vote for unity," Jonn says.

"As do I," says Lotham.

"And I," says Calla. She reaches up and rubs her orange necklace between her fingers.

"And I," says Helenea, "gladly." She smiles at Jonn, who looks surprised.

Montan is silent for a moment. He looks around the room, glancing over at the guards against the wall.

"Fine," he says. "I vote for unity. But I pray we can keep our people safe."

"As do we all," Jonn says quietly.

He turns to Motherbird. "You must vote," he says, his voice respectful.

But she turns to look at me. "Be ready," she says quietly.

I don't know what to say, so I just nod.

"The only way this allegiance will succeed,"

Motherbird says, turning her gaze to Jonn, "is if Andria does not cross over. If she returns to the faerieground, with her will come the end of us."

My jaw drops.

She can't possibly be talking about my mother.

7

Soli

Sweet,

The light one has found her way to us, right in the nick of time. She's safe. And so am I. We're worried about you, of course. We fear for your life.

We know you're strong, but it's still hard to know you're there, all alone.

I wish I was with you right now.

Motherbird told us today what happened, so now we know for sure how you chose to send Lucy and me home instead of choosing one of us to die.

I shouldn't be, but I'm grateful. I wasn't ready to die then, especially by the Crows.

But I'm angry, too. I want to think that if you'd chosen to save her instead of me, I could have fought them, and I could have been safe.

And if you had chosen to save me, then we'd be together now.

But that chance is gone, and at least we're all alive.

The Six Kingdoms gathered today. I won't tell you our decisions, because I don't know who might come across this letter, but I'll tell you I feel strong and brave.

You are in my mind, and in the light one's, and in the minds of all the faeries in your kingdom and beyond.

I know in my heart we are meant to be, Sweet. We are meant to be real, and to grow old together—if not this time, maybe next.

I will hold you in my heart until then.

yours—

K.

Soli

The words on the paper turn blurry. My hands begin to shake. I can't sit still, so I stand and pace the room.

Is Kheelan saying goodbye?

Is he in danger?

And Lucy . . . why would Lucy come back to this madness?

I try to breathe, but my chest feels tight.

I need air.

I'm allowed to leave my room these days, so I take advantage of it.

I'm almost a Crow now, it seems.

As I walk down the hallways of the Crow palace, I hold my mother's key in my hand, like every time I'm tense these days. The feeling of the cold metal digging into my skin makes me feel a little better.

I can't stop thinking about this newest letter.

I do not need rescuing; I do not need them to risk their lives. The lives of everyone in the kingdom. I chose to stay here to save them, not put them all in more danger. I have accepted my fate.

My fate is to become a Crow.

The Crows won't hurt me. They have made me one of them. They're making me stronger. They're teaching me about the faerie ways.

At the end of this hallway, there's a little nook tucked away beneath a staircase. I fold my body inside.

Tears roll down my cheeks. When I reach up to wipe them away, the key clatters to the ground.

There is a tile mosaic inlaid in the floor in this nook. It's shaped like a bird—a crow, of course, mouth open in a caw. I trace it with my finger. The tiles are cold, smooth to the touch.

Then I see it.

In the bird's gaping mouth, a tiny keyhole.

I scramble to my knees, pick up the key, and slide it into the hole.

Then I turn it.

It clicks.

And the wall in front of me begins to move.

Once the wall is gone, there's a long, dark hallway. It's deathly silent. But I'm not afraid. I want to see where my mother's key leads me.

After I walk through, the wall slides up behind me again. I walk down the damp, creepy hallway. My boots slide across the cement floor.

The cracks around the hidden entrance let in enough light to see by for a while. But after I've walked for a minute, it becomes too dark. I have to reach out my hands and touch the walls so that I can guide myself down the hall.

I find myself in a room that's lit by tiny flames in glass bowls against the wall. It's some kind of library. The room is lined with shelves of books.

The room is undeniably creepy, and I know I'm not supposed to be here. I know if Georg found out, he'd be furious.

If he even knows it's here.

Caro has never mentioned it. But then again, Caro doesn't really like books.

I can't help my curiosity. I walk deeper into the room.

Against one wall, there's an old wooden desk covered with books. Some are open, some are closed.

It reminds me of how my desk looks when I'm writing a paper for school, with everything I might need scattered around me.

There's a cup on the desk, too, and when I pick it up I see leaves—like tea, or herbs—still inside.

It's not moldy.

I think someone must have been here, not very long ago.

But who?

Next to the desk, there's a pile of seven rolled-up papers. I pick one and unroll it. It's a map of a kingdom; not the Crows', and not my own. I try another one.

In fancy writing across the top: Roseland.

I've never seen the shape of my kingdom before. It isn't shaped like a rose, of course. It's more like a

diamond. I think it must be the kingdom most central in the faerieground. It's bordered by the Crows' kingdom on one side and the Ladybirds on the other.

Then I look closer.

Tight black writing on the map marks places that are vulnerable, places where the Crows can enter without being stopped by guards, places that they can burn to the ground, places they can attack in the night.

I throw the map aside and look at the others.

All of them are the same. A detailed map, with notes on how to kill as many as possible.

The Crows plan to murder everyone. They plan to bring war across the faerieground.

And if I have become a Crow, if I plan to stay here, if I sit back and let it happen, if I eat their lies, if I train beside them, if I know about this and if I don't try to stop them—then I'm as bad as they are.

And they must know that. Keeping me here is part of their plan.

A book on the desk catches my eye. It is a black leather-bound book, heavy, with thin pages that don't feel like they were made of paper, but maybe of ground feathers.

I turn to a random page and instantly find my name.

Soledad trained for most of the morning today; she holds a bow well and sinks arrows deep.

So they are watching me.

I flip earlier in the book, find another page.

Magnus deceased; poison was effective. Calandra bereft. The halfling princess is too young to know, of course.

A bit later:

Calandra has lost control of her kingdom. Most of the faeries believe she killed Magnus.

On the next page:

The Old Ones have taken the child and given her to Andria for safekeeping. The spell blocking their knowledge of Andria will fade soon, but it worked well enough. The Queen will send the child back when she's old enough to lead; we will find her and make her one of our own. Now we wait.

I read more. It's mostly harvest reports, notations of sunrises, lists of new spells. But after years of that, I find this:

The halfling princess has returned. She is with the daughter of Andria. The pieces of our old plan have fallen into place perfectly.

So now I know.

The Crows planned this all along.

They are the ones who took me from Calandra. They tricked the Ladybirds into bringing me to Andria. I don't know why they did that, but it can't have been for a good reason.

It must have something to do with their plan.
As far as I can tell, their plan was this:

Kill my father.

Turn the people of Roseland against my mother.

Steal me away.

Make my mother crazy.

Bring me back and steal me again.

Make me a Crow.

Attack Roseland.

Attack the other kingdoms.

Kill everyone who stands in their way.

8

Lucy

*"They can't be talking about my mom,"
I whisper to Kheelan.* "Seriously. She can be weird sometimes, but she wouldn't do whatever it is they think she'd do."

We are crouching outside the clinic where my mother works, waiting for her to be done for the day. We came right away after the faerie council. I had to see what my mother was doing.

Kheelan shakes his head.

"Motherbird is never wrong, Lucy," he says. "I'm

sorry. Maybe you just haven't ever seen that side of your mother."

"It just doesn't make sense!" I say. "I know she was in the faerieground, and I know something weird happened there. But I also know she would never go back. I mean . . ."

I trail off, thinking about how my mother told us never to go into the woods, how she left offerings for the faeries, how she told me she'd angered the queen. And the necklace she used to wear, the one that matches my blue one, the green one she gave to Soli so that Soli could try to find me.

I can't imagine her going back there. I can't imagine why she'd want to.

But then I remember how she hid my necklace, how she buried it. How she seemed so odd and angry when she found out I had it.

Was it because she wanted it for herself? Was it because it was a way for her to go back?

Was she just waiting for the right time to dig it up and go into the woods?

"We need to figure out why Motherbird thinks she's a danger," Kheelan says. "She wouldn't tell us, but I could tell the other leaders knew something."

I nod. "They all looked at each other and gave me weird looks when they found out I'm her daughter," I admit. "I just don't get it."

Kheelan checks the sky, where the sun is sinking lower. "When will she be done?" he asks.

"Anytime now," I say.

And just like that, the automatic doors slide open, and my mother walks out. "There she is," I hiss, and we dive lower behind the bush.

She turns onto the sidewalk, and after she's walked halfway down the block, Kheelan and I get up and follow her. But she doesn't turn toward home at the end of the street. Instead, she walks further into town.

We follow her all the way to the Mearston Historical Society. She goes in, and we creep close to the door.

I can see her through the window. "She looks bad," I say. "Tired." Kheelan nods.

"Maybe she's just been worried about me," I say.

"Maybe," he says, but I can tell he's not convinced.

We hear loud voices coming from inside. My mother is yelling at someone I can't see.

"How could you?" she screams.

The other person replies, but I can't make out the words.

It almost seems like someone else is wearing my mother's body. She's tender and sweet. She's not a monster.

"Do you know the woman she's talking to?" Kheelan asks, leaning closer to the window.

I peer inside, craning my neck to see.

"It's Molly Murry," I say. "She works here. She's the one who helped me. She knew about my necklace."

My knees shake.

"Molly knows how to cross to the faerieground," I say.

And then we hear Molly yell, "Fine! I'll help you!"

Kheelan takes my hand and pulls me into a run. We hurry toward the woods.

Tears stream down my face.

Motherbird was right.

Soli

If I need to send a message, how can I send it?

Messages are coming to me, but I don't know how they get here. And I can't talk to anyone about them.

I don't know who I can ask.

Certainly not the king; that would be stupid.
Not any of the teachers.
Not Caro.

There's not one person here I can trust, not really.

I suppose I knew that already.

I toss and turn all night, trying to figure out what to do. How to warn the people I love, the people I'm responsible for in Roseland. Because that's the truth, isn't it? I'm still responsible for them. I'm still the queen.

But then I realize something.

Someone here in the Crows' palace is working against the Crows. Someone is bringing me the letters, even though they shouldn't. Someone is betraying their own kingdom by helping Kheelan's messages come to me.

That person, whoever they are, is my only hope.

Otherwise, the Crows will kill me, and then they'll take over the whole faerieground.

I finally doze off just as the sun is rising outside my small window. But a knock wakes me up.

Caro walks in. She narrows her eyes as soon as she sees me. "You look terrible," she says.

I'm used to her bluntness.

"I know," I say. "I couldn't sleep." I don't want to tell her why.

"What's wrong?" she asks.

I shake my head. "Just homesick, I guess," I say. And it's true. I am homesick. Not for Roseland. For my mother in Mearston. For my life in Mearston.

The truth is, sometimes this whole adventure feels like a nightmare I can't wake up from.

Caro nods. "It must be hard, all the changes in your life," she says, as if she's reading my mind. "Two months ago, you didn't even know we existed."

She's right. "Yes," I say. "It's been hard. Parts have been wonderful. But——"

I can't say any more.

She smiles. "There's a place I go," she says, cocking her

head. "When I need to get away from everyone else, when my father is being awful, you know. I think it could help you. Would you like to see it?"

Her face is relaxed, and I'm surprised by how much I like her, right now, the daughter of my captor.

"Okay," I say. "But won't we be late for class?"

She shrugs. "I miss classes all the time. If you're going to fit in around here, you might as well miss one, too."

That makes me laugh.

"Let's go," she says.

"I should dress," I say, but she shakes her head.

"Don't bother."

She takes my hand and guides me through the castle. We head up a narrow staircase, step after step, up past four or five landings. Finally, at the top, there's a small wooden door.

"Ready?" she asks. She bites her lip, and it strikes me that she's nervous.

"Does anyone else know about this place?" I ask.

She shrugs. "It must be on the castle maps," she says. "I'm sure someone knows about it. But no one ever comes here. You're the first person I ever told about it."

She opens the door.

It's as if someone built a greenhouse in one of the castle towers. Sunlight streams in. A cool breeze comes through the wide-open windows that line each wall. The room is full of potted plants and flowers, varieties I've never seen before mixed with familiar roses and lilies.

"This is beautiful," I say, dropping down to a wooden bench near the door.

"This is where I come when I need to think, when I need some time alone," Caro says.

"I can see why," I say. I gaze out the window. The tower's height lets me see the valley the castle is built in and the grounds around it. "This is really beautiful."

She smiles. "I'm glad you like it," she says.

And I do. But as I stare out at the amazing view, I remember that this beautiful place, and everything in it,

was built by faeries who want to destroy the rest of the kingdoms.

"Your face changed," Caro says. "What are you thinking about?"

She has trusted me with this secret place. Can I trust her with my problems? Can I tell her what I know about the Crows?

But who's to say she doesn't know already?
Who's to say she's not on their side?
Of course she is.

She's the princess of the Crows.

"Just thinking about home," I say.

"Would you believe I've never crossed over to the human world?" she asks. She laughs. "I've been in prisons in all seven faerie kingdoms, but I've never even seen a human home." Then she says, "What's it like there, where you're from?"

I think about Mearston.

"It's just home," I say. "It's hard to describe. I've lived there all my life—"

"Since you were two, anyway," she puts in.

"Right," I say. "As long as I have memories, anyway. It's a small town, not many buildings, not many people. I didn't have many friends, besides Lucy. We did everything together. She's like a sister to me."

I really miss Lucy.

"You must miss her," Caro says.

"I do," I say.

And she reaches over and pats my hand. "I hope you'll see her soon."

"Me too," I whisper, and a tear slides down my cheek.

"What else? What's different there?" she asks.

"Everything," I say. "We just live differently. You—"

"You mean 'we,'" Caro says. "You're a faerie, too, you know. Even half-faeries are faeries, when it comes down to it."

And I feel the weight of the wings on my back.

"It's strange, to not be human anymore," I whisper.

I've never said it out loud. That I'm not human anymore. That I'm something else.

"I'm a little jealous," Caro admits. "Sometimes I wish I'd discover something secret about myself, something no one else knows. Something that would mean I could leave this all behind. Didn't you ever want to leave your human world?"

I shake my head. "I just wanted to be with Lucy," I say. "I didn't care where I was, as long as my best friend was with me."

How quickly everything has changed.

"Now you don't have Lucy, and you don't have Kheelan," she says. Her voice is kind. "You must feel so alone."

"I do," I say. "But you've been nice to me."

"It's nice for me, too," she says. "To not be alone here."

"You're not alone, though. You have your father, and you've been here your whole life."

"Depends on what you mean when you say alone," she mutters.

Caro crosses to the windows and looks out. "I'm the king's daughter. There are no friends here for me." She looks back at me, and a spark flashes in her eyes. "Except you."

She waits for me to respond, but I don't know what to say.

Do I feel like Caro is a friend?

Yes, I do.

Do I feel like Caro is someone I trust?

I still don't know.

"We should go," I say finally. "I don't mind missing one class, but two is too many. They'll look for me."

Caro sighs, and we leave, and she locks the door behind her.

9

Lucy

We have spent two days preparing. I've helped as much as I can, but mostly I feel like I'm getting in the way. All of the faeries are so busy. They're rushing around, saddling horses and polishing weapons and packing leather bags and unrolling maps. It's like a movie about Robin Hood or something, but it's real.

They've given me a horse to ride. They asked if I knew how to ride, and I lied.

I've ridden horses before, when I was younger. Sort of. I remember going to a farm with Soli in the fall, sitting on top of a pony, having a farmer lead us in a slow circle. But I've never ridden a horse by myself. I don't even know how to climb up her tall side and settle into the saddle.

The morning that we're supposed to leave is cold and wet. Hundreds of faeries—and me—gather near the palace where Calandra used to live. Jonn is barking orders. The other leaders—Lotham, Helenea, Motherbird, Montan, and Calla—are already on their horses, yelling to their own groups.

Kheelan stands near me, holding his horse's reins and scribbling something on a ragged piece of paper.

I feel like I'm in the center of a hurricane. Everything is in motion around me and my big white horse, and I'm just watching from the middle.

Kheelan folds the piece of paper and lets out an ear-splitting whistle. A large black bird swoops down out of nowhere, and he tucks the paper into a thin band that's tied around the bird's neck. Then Kheelan whispers something, and the bird flies away.

Kheelan turns to me. "I have something for you," he says, before I can ask what the bird is doing.

He reaches into one of the bags strapped to his horse and pulls out a small leather pouch. He hands me the pouch, and it's heavy and warm in my hand.

"Open it," he says.

I do. It unrolls, and I see the handles of seven knives.

"I hope you don't need to use them," he says. "I'll try to keep you safe—not because I don't think you're strong. I do. But because you aren't trained."

I stare down at the knives. "What are they for?" I whisper.

He sighs. Then he slips one knife out of the roll.

"Like this," he says. He reaches across his body and points the knife to the left side of his chest. "Here." Then he moves it lower and to the right. "And then here."

He puts the knife back and secures the roll before putting it into the bag tied to my own horse.

I don't know what to say, so I say nothing.

I stand there, staring at him.

"It's going to be fine, Lucy," he says. He manages a small smile. "You won't need them. But you should know how to use them."

I open my mouth, but no words come out.

"Anyway," he says, "soon we'll be with Soli. And isn't that the most important part of this?"

"Maybe," I say. "But to be honest, right now I wish it was two months ago and none of this had happened."

Kheelan smiles. He reaches out and squeezes my hand. "I don't wish that," he says.

"Of course you don't," I say, shaking my head. "Two months ago, your kingdom was being led by a woman who'd gone insane from grief. Your princess had been missing for twelve years. You hadn't met the girl you'd fall in love with. The Crows were planning to attack, probably."

"That's all true," he says. "And it's true that even if I die today, meeting Soli will have made my life worthwhile."

I shake my head. "That's crazy," I say. "You guys are just teenagers. You've only known her for a little while. I mean, I believe that you love her, or whatever, but—"

"It's different here," Kheelan says, cutting me off. The smile slides from his face. "It isn't like it is where you're from. Soli and I might not be together forever, but when two faeries fall in love, it's not like when two humans do. It means more."

"Don't forget, she's only half-faerie," I mutter, instantly regretting it.

Kheelan relaxes. "I don't forget," he says. "But don't you forget, either—she's only half-human."

We stare at each other for a moment, but then a loud whistle makes us turn away.

"It is time," Jonn calls. "We ride for Roseland. And we ride for all of the faerie kingdoms."

Everyone cheers. But then the other leaders ride up next to him.

The area becomes perfectly silent.

"We know that some of us will die," Montan says, his indigo cloak smooth behind him. "The Crows will show no restraint."

"We have no choice," Calla adds from the back of her black horse, where she sits on a bright orange saddle. "This is our chance to unite the kingdom and restore peace."

Lotham, wearing a yellow cloth around his shoulders, nods. "We must work together. We must fight together."

Helenea adds, "If anyone here believes we are doing the wrong thing, it is your privilege to stay behind. But when we fight together, we survive together, and we grow together." She reaches into the bag at the side of her horse and pulls out a helmet made of some kind of shiny violet stone. "We protect each other with our numbers and with our strength," she says, before securing the helmet on her head.

The crowd cheers.

Then Motherbird, wearing a red dress, rides forward, and they are still again.

She looks out over the group and then up at the sky.

"The Crows gather," she says. "We must ride."

With that, the faeries begin to move. I climb onto my horse, and as if she knows exactly what to do, she begins to trot forward.

Motherbird rides up next to me.

"Your mother will cross over," she says.

"I know," I tell her. I haven't told her that Kheelan and I went back to Mearston to spy on my mother, but I think Motherbird knows.

"She is dangerous here," Motherbird says. Her face is kind. "But she is still your mother, and she still loves you."

I take a deep breath. "Okay," I say. "I'll try to remember that."

"You'll need to," she says.

We continue to ride, the horses moving faster.

Motherbird points to my chest. "You wear the Crows' color," she says.

The necklace, she means.

"Yes," I say. "I found it there. It helped me come back."

"Keep it safe, and it will keep you safe," she says. "But do not let anyone take it from you. No one. Understand?"

"I understand."

"If it falls into the wrong hands, it will devastate us," she tells me. "All of us."

"Okay," I say. "I get it." Then I think about it. "Do you want to take it? Would it be safer with you?"

She smiles. "Heavens, no," she says. "I won't live through this. But you will. You are the person who can protect it. You are the Light One, and you are here to help us fight against the dark."

I don't understand, but now isn't the time for explanations.

"Okay," I say quietly. I don't know if she can even hear me, the crowd of horses and faeries is so loud.

"Be careful, Lucy," Motherbird says. "But be brave."

Soli

If I want to get a message to Kheelan before they come for me, I need to find out who's helping him get messages to me.
So after our morning classes, I hide.

I hide under my bed and wait, just me and the cobwebs and the dust bunnies.

It's boring, of course, and I start to feel claustrophobic and strange under the bed. I start to feel like a prisoner, even more than I already do.

There's a knock, and I stiffen.

The door swings open. I recognize Caro's boots.

"Soli?" she says.

I don't say anything. I stay under the bed, silent as I can be.

She walks closer, and I hear the creak of the window being opened.

The sound of beating wings enters the room.

"Good bird," Caro says.

I hear the wings again, leaving, and then she closes the window.

Paper rustles, and then she walks back to the door.

But she doesn't leave.

"I know you're here," she says, her voice low and calm.

I don't say anything. I try to keep my breathing as quiet as possible.

"Don't make me look under the bed, Soli," she says.

I sigh. Then I crawl out.

She doesn't bother trying to explain. She just reaches out and hands me a folded piece of paper.

"We have a problem," she says.

"You read it?" I ask, but I know it doesn't matter.

I open the paper.

Sweet—

It is dawn, and we are flying toward you.

yours—

K.

I look at Caro. "So it was you the whole time," I say.

A smile twists on her face. "Didn't you know?"

"No," I say. "I didn't."

"It's in my name," she tells me, crossing her arms across her chest. "Caro, the Betrayer."

Part 3

Soli

"I'm sorry I read your letters," Caro says. We are in her greenhouse tower room, watching out the window for approaching faeries.

I shrug. "It's okay," I say.

And it is. At first I felt embarrassed, but I have nothing to be ashamed of. I haven't done anything wrong.

"Are you going to tell my father?" she asks quietly. "I know he would listen to you. He'd be furious with me, but he'd believe you."

"Of course not," I say. "Why would I tell him? It would get me in trouble, too."

Receiving letters from Roseland? Knowing that faeries from my kingdom were coming to rescue me? I'd never tell him.

"Because it could get me out of the way," she says. "If you told him, he'd banish me or something. And you could be the princess here, and eventually the queen."

"I don't want to be the princess here," I say. I look around the room. "I mean, it's beautiful and everything. And most people have been kind to me since I decided to stay. But—"

"But the Crows are terrible," she says.

We stare at each other.

I nod.

"You think I'm terrible, too," she says.

I sigh. "Caro, I don't know what to think about you," I say, and it's true.

Caro, the Betrayer.

So far, she's betrayed everyone, over and over again.

I don't understand her.
But I do like her.

"I understand," she says, her face looking hurt.

"I don't think you do," I say. "I mean, you've betrayed everyone. Just like your name says. But I do like you. And I do believe that you weren't trying to get me in trouble or anything like that."

She looks up at me. "Why would you get in trouble? You weren't the one betraying the Crows. You've probably never done anything wrong in your life."

Then a twinkle glints in her eye.
"Yet," she says.

I smile. "Yet," I say.

We watch out the window for a while longer.

"When they come, whose side are you on?" I ask finally.

Caro shrugs. "I'm on my own side, like always," she says.

I don't know what that means.

Is her side my side?

Or is her side whichever side doesn't get her killed?

She can tell that's what I'm trying to understand.

"I'm on the side of winning," she says finally. "But I don't know who will win this."

We stare out at the lush forest past the valley.

"I wonder what my mother would have done, if she were here," I say. "I mean, as the queen. Not my other mother, my human mother. The faerie one."

"I don't remember my mother," Caro says. "It must be interesting to have two."

"I don't know much about Calandra," I admit. "What happened to your mother?"

She is silent, and I feel bad. I shouldn't have asked something so personal.

"She ran away," she says finally. "She ran back to the humans."

She looks me in the eye and adds, "My mother is Andria."

Soli

Caro tells me.

Three years before Calandra gave birth to me, her older sister, Andria, came to the faerieground.

She had been obsessed with faeries for years—she knew they could be reached through Willow Forest, outside Mearston. She wanted, more than anything, to cross over and meet them.

She wanted to become one.

She finally crossed over, with help from the Mearston Historical Society.

And when she did, the first person she met was the young Crow prince, Georg.

They fell in love, even though Andria was human and Georg was a faerie. They were married. And then Georg's father died, and Georg became king, and Andria became queen.

Caro was born a little more than a year after Andria came to the faeries.

And a few months after that, Calandra came to save her sister. Andria was sent home, and Calandra stayed. A year later, I was born.

Caro never knew she had a half-sister until Lucy arrived in the faerieground.

Looking at Caro now, I can't believe I didn't notice it before. She and Lucy have the same coloring, the same quick grin, the same mischievous eyes.

"So you're my cousin," I say. "Our mothers were sisters."

She nods. "Yes," she says. "And I'm sorry for—for everything I've done to you."

I can't say it's okay.

"I forgive you," I say finally. "I don't know if I would have done differently, if I were you."

She laughs. "Of course you would have."

"So you don't remember Andria at all?" I ask.

Caro shakes her head. "No. What is she like?"

I think about Andria.

"She was like a mother to me," I say. "A second mother." Then I laugh. "A third mother, I guess."

"She was kind?" Caro asks.

I nod. "Always. She protected me. I always believed that she loved me."

"I wonder if she loves me," Caro whispers.

A tear slips from her eye, but before I can say anything to try to make her feel better, she leaps up and crosses the room.

"I want to give you something," she says. "My mother's journal." She pulls a book from beneath a bench.

"From when she was here?" I ask.

Caro nods. "She wrote in it every day. Maybe you'd like to read it."

"What's it like?" I ask.

She shrugs. "I haven't read it," she admits. "Honestly, I've been so mad at her for leaving. And I don't really like reading anyway."

I think about the shelves of books in her room, the books I've devoured since I came to the Crows.

"I'd love to look at it," I say. "Thank you."

She hands me the book. And then we sit, and watch, and wait.

Lucy

We ride all day. By nightfall, I'm starting to have a hard time feeling my legs. Kheelan rides effortlessly. I envy his confidence, his skills.

He catches me staring. I feel myself blush and look away.

I think about how Kheelan and I met—locked together in a cell. "Remember when we met?" I ask. "Why were you in the cell?"

He laughs. "My father was mad at me," he says. "Wanted to teach me a lesson, I suppose."

"Why was he mad?"

He shrugs. "I was always disobeying him," he explains. "Trying to get over to the human world, trying to explore the faerieground, going out of the boundaries of Roseland."

"And he wasn't okay with that?" I ask, surprised. Jonn seems like an adventurer.

"He was Queen Calandra's personal guard," Kheelan says with a smile. "I was an embarrassment to him. So once in a while, he'd throw me in the cells."

He looks up at his father, riding far in front of us. "I guess things have changed," he adds quietly.

A cramp seizes my leg. "How long before we take a break?" I ask. "I—"

He nods. "Another hour or so." He makes his horse slow down, matching my pace. "Do you think you can make it?"

"Yes," I say.

I think we must be far beyond the boundaries of Roseland. "Where are we?" I ask.

"The Equinox kingdom," Kheelan says. "Crow land."

"This gives me the creeps," I tell him, looking around in the darkness. Even the trees seem angrier here.

"Try to take your mind off it," he says. "Why don't you tell me how you first came to the faerieground?"

"Don't you know?" I ask, and he shakes his head. "Soli sent me here by mistake."

He laughs. "How did she do that?"

"She made a wish in the woods," I say quietly. "It seems like so long ago, but really, it was only a few weeks. How weird."

"What was her wish?"

I sigh. Then I tell him the whole story: how Soli had a crush on Jaleel, and how I promised I'd talk to him for her. And how, when I talked to him, I saw what she saw. And I liked him, too. And how I let him kiss me, and then, at school, how I kissed him again.

How Soli saw.

And then I tell him about the fight in the woods. How I chased her into the forest and begged her to forgive me.

And then, finally, how she wished me away, and I found myself in the faerieground, all alone and afraid.

"And that's when they put me in the cell, and then I met you," I say.

"So you kissed the boy she thought she loved," he says.

"Not loved," I say, laughing. "She just thought he was nice. He talked to her. He made her feel important."

"That makes sense," he says. "So why did you kiss him?"

I shrug.

"I guess he made me feel important, too," I say quietly. "Does that make sense?"

"It does," he says.

"And then when I went back to school, I couldn't believe I'd let a boy come between us," I add. "I mean, my best friend liked him, and I kissed him. I feel really awful about it."

Kheelan smiles. "Everyone makes mistakes," he says. "And I have to admit, I'm not sorry. I do believe Soli would have crossed over someday no matter what, but I'm glad I met her."

"I'm glad, too," I say.

"I hope we aren't too late to save her," he says. "I hope—"

But he stops. Then he straightens his shoulders and rides ahead quickly, leaving me alone.

12

Andria

Day 4

The faeries are not what I expected. They're darker. Meaner.

More interesting.

I want to be one of them.

I want to be more than human.

I want to belong here.

There must be a way to become faerie. I can't really ask anyone, but I've hinted at it, and so far no one seems to know anything.

Georg knows my secret wish, though.

It's funny, the different ways people talk about Georg. Some call him cold, mean, rude. Others call him smart, wise beyond his years, the sure successor to the Crow crown.

Me? I call him the most beautiful creature I've ever seen.

And he's the only person I've met who hasn't treated me like an outsider.

I know I don't belong here, but I want to belong here. I want to belong with him, and I think he wants that, too.

He asked me to take a walk in the woods with him tomorrow night, and I'm going to. He said he might have information that could help me.

So far he's the only one who wants to help me.

I understand. The others here have no reason to want me to stay.

But he's helped me. He convinced his father to find a room for me. He convinced everyone I wasn't a spy.

And daily, he finds me, to sit and talk and laugh for a while, so I don't feel too alone.

He knows I don't want to go home, not ever.

Is it crazy to think that Georg and I might have a future together?

Is it crazy to hope for that?

I don't know if I'll be able to sleep tonight, knowing that we have plans for tomorrow.

Is it a date?

Maybe I can think of it like that, secretly. Just for myself.

A date with a prince in the faerieground woods.

Soli

The first thing that catches my eye is the banners of color coming toward the castle, shining bright in the distance.

Then the horses.

Then the noise, far away, of yelling and music.

The noise of war.

Caro is asleep next to me on the bench, and I shake her awake.

"Look," I say. "They're coming."

She gazes out the window. Dawn has broken, and it looks like most of the faerieground is headed fast into the Crows' valley.

"How long do we have before they're at the castle?" I ask.

She shrugs. "Maybe fifteen minutes."

"How long before your father knows they're here?"

She narrows her eyes at me and laughs. "Don't be stupid," she says, that familiar meanness creeping back into her voice. "He knew they were coming before we did. He probably knew they were coming before they did."

"What should we do?" I ask, stumbling to my feet.

She slowly stands. "Let's go downstairs," she says. "I don't want them to come looking for us."

"Who?" I ask, and she gives me that look again.

"The army," she tells me. "Come on."

In the throne room, Georg stares out the window at the valley. He looks fearless, strong, frightening. Mikael, his guard, stands behind him.

"Set the Crows loose," Georg says, turning to Mikael. "Let the big birds have some fun."

"As you wish," Mikael says, and bows respectfully.

Georg turns to me. "I believe I have you to thank for this turn of events," he says, but he doesn't look angry. He looks hungry. "It's been years in the making, but finally, they've found a reason strong enough to threaten us."

My stomach turns with fear.

"You'll both fight in the front lines," he says, walking toward the door. "You have the training and knowledge it will take, thanks to your instructors here. Find your armor and your weapons and join the army in the courtyard."

Then he stops, turns back to me.

"Once they see you're on our side," he says, "they will know there's no hope. They will surrender to me, and the Crows will finally rule the faerieground, the way we were destined to."

I don't say anything. I have to pretend to go along with this. He thinks I'm one of them, and if I make him believe otherwise, this cruel man won't hesitate to have me killed.

"Are you ready?" he asks.

"Of course we are," Caro says. "Come, Soli."

She begins to pull me out of the room, but I stop. "I have one request, sir," I say, bowing my head.

"What is it?" Georg asks.

"I would like to wear my crown," I say. "If they see me as their queen turned against them, rather than a simple girl, I think they'll be more likely to give up. Don't you?"

A spark flashes in the king's eyes. "Brilliant," he says.

"I'll have your crown returned to your room while you dress."

I bow and follow Caro before I can say anything else.

I don't know where this idea came from, but I think I need my crown. Of course King Georg knows its power, but he doesn't think I know, and he thinks I'm a Crow now.

He thinks I'd never do anything to fight against him.
He thinks I'm stupid.
He thinks I'd fight my own people.

He thinks wrong.

13

Lucy

It starts before we reach the clearing.
Huge, black birds swoop down toward us, darkening the
sky. The first line of horses rushes into the valley anyway.

"Charge!" Jonn screams. "Bows to the sky. Get those
birds on the ground!"

Everyone follows his command.

In front of me, Kheelan pulls out his bow, still riding.
He puts two arrows to the bow and frees them, sending
two of the birds straight to the ground. Then he takes out
two more arrows and repeats the action.

The shouting of all the faeries grows louder. Horses stumble and fall to the ground as the birds attack their riders. Birds sink from the sky, but I'm sure there are far more of them than there are of us.

This isn't what I expected.

It's much worse.

I pull on the reins, bringing my horse to a halt, at the same moment that a bird soars straight into Kheelan's horse's face, poking at its eyes.

Kheelan leaps off, pointing an arrow straight at the bird's heart. He lets it go and the bird falls, but the horse has already been blinded.

I ride closer. "Are you okay?" I ask. There's so much fear in my voice, I'm embarrassed. "Get on my horse," I add.

He shakes his head. "They are looking for me," he yells. "Get away, Lucy! You're not safe near me."

But I don't know where to go. Nowhere seems safe.

"Go!" Kheelan yells again. He looks up at me, shading his eyes. "Find Motherbird. And Lucy, put your necklace away!"

I look down. The necklace has found its way out of my shirt, so I quickly tuck it in.

Then I turn my horse around and head toward the back of the group, looking for Motherbird and the other Ladybirds.

Finally, I see the flush of red bringing up the rear of our army.

As I ride closer, I can see that the Ladybirds' arrows shoot red smoke toward the sky.

I see a brush of red riding down the clearing.

A hand grabs my arm, and I turn. It's Motherbird.

"Follow me," she says.

My horse turns in her direction, following her without me guiding it.

I ride alongside the Ladybirds as we head toward the castle grounds. The birds are still coming fast and furious, but the Ladybirds fight them away effortlessly.

Just as we enter the castle grounds, Motherbird pulls me behind a boulder in a garden filled with black-petaled tulips.

"Are you afraid?" she asks.

I shake my head, although we both know that's a lie.

"Is my mother here already?" I ask.

She shakes her head.

There are screams coming from the front of the line.

"The Crows have come," she says. And I know she means the faeries, not the birds. Although I'm not sure what difference there is. Maybe the birds are the faeries, and the faeries are the birds.

"You need to protect that necklace if we want a chance at winning this war," she says. "Do you know what it means?"

"No," I say. "I found it—"

"In the Crows' nest," she finishes for me. "I know. It's been there for a very long time."

She pulls her own pendant out from beneath her cloak. It's the same as the one I wear, except that it's a deep ruby red.

"Touch it," she says, stretching the necklace toward me.

I reach out. It's warm from being tucked next to her body.

As my hand closes around the necklace, I begin to see images flashing through my head. Faeries, sitting together around a long wooden table. Then an argument. Then a war. Then—the seven necklaces, one in each color of the rainbow, each one around a different throat.

Motherbird gently pries my fingers away from the necklace, and I open my eyes.

"When the kingdom was split, we were each given a key," she says. "All seven keys can make the kingdom whole again. But the necklaces must be whole—they must all be safe."

I frown. "If we have all seven, can't we just put them together?"

"No," she says. "The necklaces are bound to their owners—the rulers of the seven kingdoms. Georg must agree."

"I understand," I say.

"Good," she says. "Now we must return to the fight. And you must stay safe, so please, Lucy, stay behind me. I know what to expect, but fate can always change."

The Crow army is pouring out of the castle.

I pull my horse behind Motherbird's and follow her forward.

Shouting—and the piercing whistles of speedy arrows—comes from the two armies as they meet on the grounds before us.

I look up, shielding my face. I want to see what the enemy looks like.

The Crow warriors are dressed in black, with black metal armor and black metal helmets. They are far better protected than the army from the other kingdoms.

And on the front line, right in the middle of the charging army, I see a helmetless girl, wearing a crown, and she has the face of my best friend.

Andria

Day 426

I promised to keep it a secret, but I can't. I told the one person who can't tell anyone in the kingdom. I'm too happy to keep it to myself. I had to tell her, even though I know she won't understand.

I miss Calandra, I do—I think of her often. It's true that we haven't always seen eye to eye. The opposite, really. But she's my sister, my lifelong best friend.

My lifelong worst enemy, sometimes.

But my sister, all the same.

I've known her for nineteen years, since my mother first held her out to me.

When we were small, I never kept a secret from Calandra, and she never kept a secret from me. Our lives were open books. We shared everything. After all, I'm only a year older than she is—we really grew up together, spent all our time together.

Of course, all that changed when I learned about the faeries.

How could she think this place didn't exist?

And worse, how could she think it would be a place full of sadness, or badness, or anything other than a perfect place full of happiness?

Perhaps, as the new queen, I am biased. Maybe after a hundred years here I will see some dark side to the faerieground. Perhaps I won't always feel like I stumbled into paradise.

I almost wish I could bring Calandra here to tell her, to show her. Faced with the beauties of this place, she would have to understand. She would have to see what I have always seen.

And, like I said, I do miss her.

So I had to send my sister a message.

I had to tell her she was going to be an aunt.

I had to tell her that a half-faerie child is growing inside me.

And if Georg and I find the right spell before she's born, the baby I carry will be all faerie—and so will I.

15

Soli

My crown is heavy on my head as I face the faerie army.

"Don't hurt anyone," I whisper to Caro.

She narrows her eyes. "I'll try," she says.

The Crow armor is light, like feathers. It looks like metal, but is stronger and almost weightless on my body. My backpack is twice as heavy as the full-body armor I'm wearing.

I draw my bow and aim it up, careful to direct it in a way that it'll miss any faerie—or human—marks.

"Don't worry about hitting a bird," Caro says. "They're all ours."

I look around, hoping no one can hear us. The sky is dark with birds.

"Are you sure?" I say. "Couldn't some of them belong to the Ladybirds?"

Caro snorts. "No way," she says. "Look at them. Crows, all of them."

Then we fight.

Caro and I work well together, and we're sneaky. Together, we disarm other Crows. We take down the circling birds. We never once hit someone from the other army.

"There are so many of them," I whisper.

"All six of the other kingdoms are here," Caro tells me. "You can tell by the colors."

"What do you mean?"

"Red, orange, yellow, green, indigo, and purple," Caro says. "We're the blue ones, but no Crow has worn blue for generations."

The rainbow of soldiers spreads out before us. The Crows aren't letting them get any closer to the castle.

But as we fight, I start to see that the other faeries recognize me. They truly do think I'm fighting against them.

I start to feel afraid.

And then a shower of arrows comes our way.

In a flash, Mikael dives toward us, knocking Caro and me to the ground. The arrows miss, but only by a millimeter. They hit Mikael instead.

He grunts in pain, but stands up anyway.

"Are you okay?" I ask, but he pushes me aside and walks away.

Then I hear my name.

"Soli!" cries the familiar voice.

It's Kheelan.

But I don't see him.

Then there's a break in the crowd, and he rushes toward me on foot.

He sees me.

He stops.

In the middle of the war, he stares at me.

Then he points his bow in my direction, and the arrow flies toward me.

Lucy

"Your friend fights there," Motherbird says, watching me as I stare at Soli.

"I see that," I say.

"She fights next to the Crows," Motherbird says.

"Yes," I say. "I get it." But I can't believe it.

The crowds close between us, and I can't see Soli anymore.

"We will keep you safe if you go toward her," Motherbird says.

And I do. I don't have a choice but to move closer. I

trust that the Ladybirds will keep me safe, covering me as I head closer to the front.

I have to get Soli's necklace and make sure it's still unbroken.

If she's fighting for the Crows, then the necklace needs to be safe with the people of Roseland.

I don't need to be told what to do. I just know. And Motherbird tells me to go, that they will follow and protect me.

I can't believe she's fighting for them, with Caro by her side. Caro, the Betrayer, shoulder to shoulder with my best friend. Caro, the girl who took me away from the safe haven of the Ladybirds.

I guess I've been replaced, and so has Roseland.

Soli comes into my view at the same time that I hear someone shout her name.

"Soli!"

It's Kheelan.

I stop in my tracks. But I don't see him in the crowd.

I push closer, closer. I see Soli looking for Kheelan. But whether it's to kiss him or shoot him, I don't know.

Then I see Kheelan.

He stops when he sees her, wearing the Crow armor and pointing a Crow bow into the approaching army.

And before I can say anything, or go any closer, he raises his own bow and shoots.

An arrow streaks toward her at the speed of light.

And as it does, I know in my heart that Soli is still on our side.

"No!" I scream.

Andria

Day 793

Calandra is here.

I can't believe it.

My sister, here.

I can't believe she was able to cross over. It took me years to figure it out, and she comes just months after receiving my message that Caro was born?

Caro is the thing that reminds me, daily, that this life isn't a dream.

Seeing Calandra here reminded me that my old life

wasn't a dream, either. It was a real life, and a real place, and real people.

When she met Georg today, she seemed horrified. Like he was some kind of monster. You'd think she'd be excited to meet her sister's husband, the father of her sister's new baby.

She held Caro, but didn't seem to love her.

If only the spells had worked. If only I was a pure faerie now, instead of the human queen. Then she'd see. She'd see how much I've changed, being here. She'd see what a wonderful place it is.

I can't believe it. She didn't even understand how much I love Georg.

She went straight up to him in the throne room and told him to release me. That it wasn't safe here for me and that I needed to go home where I belonged.

I laughed, then. Home? Where I belonged?

I belong here. This is my home.

Georg laughed, too, of course. He knows I belong here. He knows I love it here.

And he told her that.

He told her that he could have chosen any faerie girl to marry, but he chose me. And that I chose him. And that our daughter—beautiful, sweet Caro—was proof of our love.

He found Calandra a room to sleep in, even though I said we should send her back. He said he wanted her to be comfortable.

Tonight, he told me his plan. He thinks she will not go without trying to save me. And so we can use her presence here to put a grand scheme into place. Something he has wanted for years.

To bring the faerieground together, with him as the king.

I told him I'd do anything he asked me to do to make the plan work.

He brushed the hair out of my face with his rough fingers, smiled at me, and kissed me gently. And then he told me what I'd have to do. What my part of the plan would be.

I will have to leave. And it may be years before I can come back.

16

Soli

Kheelan's eyes don't leave mine as his arrow grazes my hair, landing behind me.

I hear the thud of a Crow's body hitting the ground.

I let out a long breath.

He wasn't aiming at me.

He trusts me.

He knows I'm still me.

He knows I'm not one of them.

I drop my bow and run to him. He kisses me, wraps his arms around me.

"You're here," I say.

"You're safe," he says.

We cling together in the middle of the chaos.

I know I'm supposed to pretend to be on the Crow side, but I can't. Not now. Not with Kheelan standing before me.

Lucy rushes up to us, and I hug her. "You're here," I say. "I'm not glad you're in this, but I'm glad you're here."

"Me too," she says. Then she looks at Kheelan. "We have so much to tell you."

Caro steps up next to me. "We need to move," she says. "Now."

Both Kheelan and Lucy narrow their eyes at her.

"It's okay," I say. "I trust her. I think."

Kheelan raises an eyebrow. "Trust her? Caro the Betrayer?"

Caro rolls her eyes. "You don't have to trust me," she says. "But we have to go. Now."

She points to the sky.

Clouds are darkening the entire bowl of the sky, gathering quickly, as if a horrible storm is coming.

"She's here," Lucy whispers.

Around us, the Crows and the other faeries stop fighting. Everyone stares at the sky.

Motherbird runs to us. I've never seen such an old woman move so quickly. She runs like a fawn.

"Andria is here," she says. She looks at Lucy, and she looks at Caro. Then she says, "Your mother has returned."

Lucy stares at Caro. "Your mother?" Lucy says.
Caro's nostrils flare. "Our mother," she says. "Yes."

Lucy takes a deep breath and then nods. "Of course,"

she says. The flicker of a smile crosses her face, and she says, "I've always wanted a sister."

"Why is she here?" I ask, but no one answers me.

"Hurry," Motherbird says. "Seek shelter."

"I know where we can go," Caro tells us.

"Be safe," Motherbird says. Then she is swallowed up by the crowd of fighting faeries.

The sky continues to darken.

"Fall back!" we hear. It is Jonn's voice. "Fall back!"

Part 4

Lucy

I follow Caro and Soli up a long staircase. Kheelan is behind us, making sure no one else knows where we're going.

At the top of the stairs is a room full of flowers. Up there, it's hard to believe a battle still rages down below.

Outside the window, the sky keeps getting darker.

We just stand there, watching.

"This is so scary," I say finally, breaking the silence.

Caro nods.

"I'm not afraid," Kheelan says. "How much damage

can one human woman do? Andria won't defeat all of these warriors."

Soli frowns. "I'm afraid, too," she says. "I've been reading Andria's journal, from when she was here. And—"

She looks at me and bites her lip. Then she says, "I'm sorry, Lucy, for what I'm going to say."

"It's okay," I say. "I think I already know. You're going to say that she was crazy. Is crazy."

Soli nods slowly. "It's like she lost her mind," she says. "She was so obsessed with the faerieground. And when she got here and Georg fell in love with her—"

"She got even crazier," I finish.

Soli and I stare at each other.

"But what I don't understand is why it's so dangerous for her to be here," Caro says. "What's the big deal?"

I lean on the windowsill. "I don't get that part either," I admit. "But Motherbird—"

Just then, there's a gentle knock on the door.

Caro opens it, and Motherbird herself walks in.

"We were just talking about you," Soli says, smiling.

"I know," Motherbird says. She settles herself onto a

bench. She seems tired. "I came to answer the questions that I know the four of you have."

"Tell us why my mother is so dangerous," I say, sitting down next to Motherbird.

She sighs. "She herself isn't dangerous," she says slowly. "What is dangerous here, as always, is Georg."

"So why does it matter if Andria is here?" Kheelan asks.

"She was beloved in the kingdom," Motherbird says. "She wanted to be faerie more than anything else in the world, and she would—and will—stop at nothing to become the faerie queen of the Crows."

"Is there a way for her to become a faerie?" Soli asks quietly.

Motherbird nods.

"What?" Caro asks. "I thought that was impossible. Everyone has always said it was impossible."

"I know you asked to become full faerie," Motherbird tells her, and Kheelan and Soli and I stare at Caro.

"You did?" Kheelan asks. "Why?"

Caro snorts. "Well, wouldn't you try everything?"

she asks. "If you were half-human, I mean? And everyone knew it?"

"No," Soli says. She reaches over and pats Caro's hand. "But I understand. Not quite fitting into either world."

"Is that why you're the Betrayer?" Kheelan asks. "Because you would try anything, betray anyone, say anything, trying to find out how to become full faerie?"

Caro rolls her eyes. "This isn't really about me," she says.

"What it takes to become full faerie is known," Motherbird says.

Caro stares at her. "No, it isn't," she says.

"Yes, it is," Motherbird says gently.

"Everyone has always told me it was impossible," Caro says. "Impossible. Completely impossible. Out of the question."

"I know," Motherbird says. "And the fact remains, everyone has lied to you."

She gestures out the window. "She's here," she says calmly.

The five of us stare down at the battleground.

The crowd of faeries slowly parts, and a figure in blue makes her way through them.

"My mother," Caro whispers.

"She's so small," I say. "She doesn't look like she could hurt anyone."

"I don't think she wants to hurt anyone," Motherbird says carefully. "She may not want to be evil, but it won't stop her, when it comes down to it. She wants to be faerie—to be the faerie queen of the Equinox kingdom—more than she wants to be good."

"So what is the secret?" I ask. "What makes a human faerie?"

Motherbird sighs. "The reason we keep this a secret," she says, "is because of what it takes—what the magic requires."

"Are you going to tell us, or not?" Kheelan asks. "I can tell it's important for us to know."

Motherbird nods. "You're right," she says. "What it takes—what the magic demands—is the kingdom's necklace—the source of its power—and the blood of a halfling."

Soli

The blood of a halfling.

"That means me," I say.

"Or me," Caro says.

We stare at each other.

Motherbird stares out the window.

"Andria is in the palace now," Kheelan says, gazing down into the courtyard, still full of faeries. "We need to protect you both."

"We need to protect all of you," Motherbird says. She stands up. "Stay here."

Then she leaves, her red coat trailing behind her.

"Should I go talk to her?" Lucy asks. "To my mother?"

Kheelan shakes his head. "Wearing the Equinox pendant? No," he says.

"I don't understand something," Caro admits. "Why would it matter if a necklace were part of the spell? I understand why it's frightening that the spell needs a halfling. But a necklace is just a necklace. I don't even know what they're talking about."

"That's not true," Lucy says. "There are seven necklaces."

I nod. "Roseland's is part of my crown," I explain. "But Andria had it before that."

Lucy pulls a blue pendant out of her shirt. "And this one belongs to the Crows."

Caro narrows her eyes. "I've never seen that before," she says.

"It was lost," Kheelan says. "Or so the story goes."

"I found it in a closet the day Soli sent us home," Lucy says. "So I guess it was lost. But not lost that well."

Then I understand.

The Crows thought their own pendant was lost, so they sent Andria home with Roseland's.

"They knew she needed one of the necklaces for part of the spell," I say slowly. "That's why Andria had mine."

Lucy shivers. "That gives me the creeps," she says.

"But they know I have it now," I say.

"Yes," Caro says. "You even convinced my father to give it back to you. They definitely know you have it."

"They?" Kheelan repeats. "Your people, Caro."

"Stop it," I say.

Kheelan's eyes open wide.

"She's not always right," I add, "but now she's on our side. She can't betray us. She's a halfling, too."

Caro and I stare at each other.
We are both not quite human, not quite faerie.
At least someone understands.

"You're the only halfling at risk, Soli," Kheelan says. "If they just needed any halfling, they would've killed Caro when she was a baby."

And I know he is right.

"She couldn't have," Lucy says quietly, looking at her half-sister. "She loved you too much."
Then she looks at me. "But she loves you, too, Soli."

I laugh. "Loves me enough to raise me up until she could send me back to the faerieground," I mutter. "Loves me enough to kill me."

"I won't betray you," Caro whispers. She reaches over and squeezes my hand.

Outside the window, the faerie army retreats. The sky is a deep, dark shade of blue.

We hear shouting from downstairs, but we can't understand the words.

I hear Andria's voice, and Georg's.

And Motherbird's.

And then it is silent.

"Motherbird is gone," Kheelan whispers. He points to the window. "They killed her."

Outside, a red bird soars past the castle and into the sky.

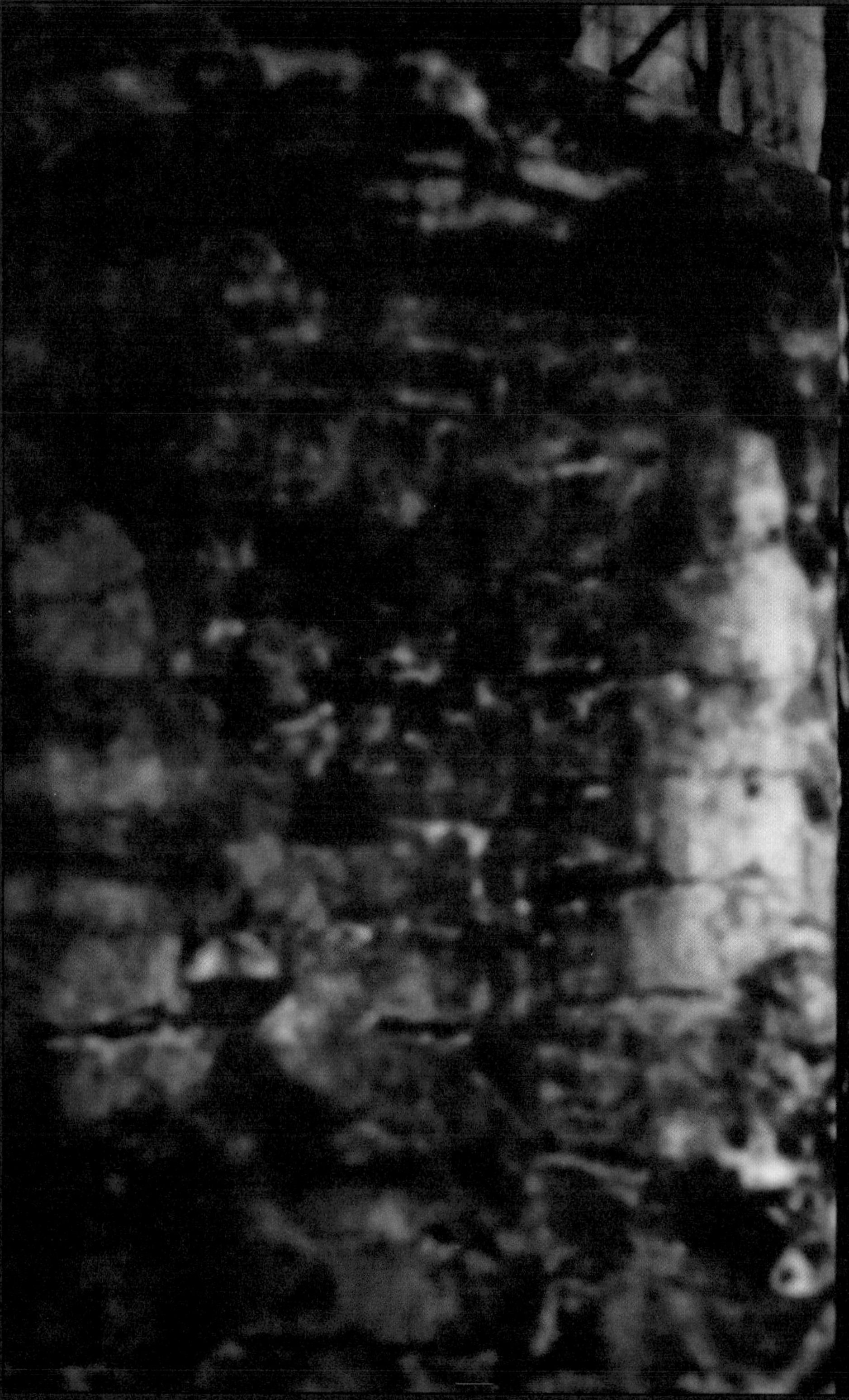

Lucy

The battle is over. Our armies have retreated. So the four of us head back to Roseland as soon as night falls.

Caro doesn't stop to pack anything in her room. She just leaves, carrying only her bow and arrow. She doesn't turn her head in the direction of our mother's voice in the throne room, the sound of our mother laughing with Caro's father. She doesn't even turn around when we reach the gardens at the edge of the castle grounds.

She just keeps moving forward.

We have to walk for two days. Kheelan feeds us with

animals he kills. The meat doesn't taste like any meat I've ever known. He doesn't tell us what kind of animal it comes from.

We don't talk much, the four of us. I don't think any of us know what the plan is.

At nightfall on the second day, we hear footsteps coming from the path ahead of us. Kheelan and Caro immediately draw their bows.

"Stay back," Kheelan whispers to me and Soli.

But Soli draws her bow, too, and I wrap my hand around the hilt of one of my knives.

The figure steps out from behind a tree.

It's Jonn.

"Father," Kheelan says, lowering his weapon.

"Son," Jonn says. "I'm glad to see you." He looks at the rest of us and bows when he sees Soli. "And your majesty," he adds. "Your people will be so relieved."

Soli smiles. "I'm glad to see you, too," she says.

Jonn leads us the rest of the way back to Roseland. At the palace, Jonn and Kheelan go to their rooms in the wing where the guards live, and Soli, Caro, and I walk up

the stairs to the rooms where Queen Calandra lived. We fall onto the soft couches and sleep.

When I wake up, a whole day has passed. Caro and Soli are gone.

They've left a note:

Come to the throne room when you can.

I splash water on my face and head downstairs.

When I open the heavy doors, I see Kheelan, Soli, and Caro gathered at the table where I met the other faerie leaders before the war began.

It looks like a study table in the library at school, the way they're hunched together over books and papers, but I know they're not cramming for a quiz or researching an essay.

Not for the first time, I think this adventure is too much for me.

I used to be a normal girl, and here I am, the daughter of a woman who wants to murder my best friend as part of a spell to become a faerie queen.

Not for the first time, I wish I'd never come to this place.

Soli

We've only been back at the palace in Roseland for a day, but already I feel overwhelmed.

I'm no queen.
But I know I have to act like one.

So as soon as I wake up after napping for a few hours, I go to Jonn and Kheelan's rooms. Caro and Lucy are still asleep.

Kheelan answers the door, and his eyes soften when

he sees me. "Hello," he says, pulling me by the hand into their main room.

But I pull my hand back. When his face looks hurt, I try to look reassuring.

"I'm here on business," I say.

He knows that his father is the Queen's main advisor. "I'll get my father," he says immediately.

Jonn comes out of his room, looking tired. Who knows if he even slept.

"Hello, Queen Soledad," he says, bowing lightly. "I hope you were able to rest."

"Hi, Jonn," I say. "I need your help. I need to figure out what to do next."

We sit down at their modest dining table. Kheelan serves me a cup of tea. It tastes like rose petals and grass.

"Have you heard about Motherbird?" Jonn asks.

I shake my head. "I hadn't heard. But we thought—"

"She is gone," Jonn says. "Another Ladybird, Elsain, has taken her place."

"Was it Andria?" I whisper.

"No," Jonn says. "Georg. But I'm sure Andria had something to do with it."

"Is Elsain on our side?" I ask.

He nods. "Motherbird knew this was coming, of course," he says. "She was prepared, and she chose her successor carefully."

"Motherbird was amazing," I say quietly.

Jonn smiles. "She was," he says. Then his face darkens. "But I'll never understand why she brought you to Andria, knowing what we know now."

"It was a spell," I tell him. "I read about it in a book I found in the Crow palace."

Then I tell him about the secret room and the book where the Crows had recorded the details of their plan.

Jonn shakes his head when I'm done. "They're worse than we thought," he says.

"They're evil," Kheelan adds.

"They just want power," I say. "And they have a terrible king."

"Was he awful to you?" Kheelan asks, reaching across the table to take my hand.

I think.

Was he awful?

He fed me, clothed me, trained me.

He praised me.

He trusted me.

He was cruel to his daughter.

He gladly would have killed me.

"I don't trust him," I say finally. "At all."

"And with Andria back, there's not a Crow in the world we can trust," Jonn says.

Kheelan shakes his head. "We can trust Caro," he says. "She's a betrayer, but—"

"But she's been waiting to find the right side to be on," I finish for him.

We smile at each other across the table.

"So what is your plan?" Jonn asks me. "What do we do?"

"I came here to ask you that," I admit. "I need help figuring it out."

"What does your blood tell you?" he asks. "What do you hear when you listen?"

And while it's a strange question, I know what he means.

I close my eyes and listen.

I listen to my heart.

I hear my heartbeat, pulsing my blood through my body.

I feel my veins thriving.

The faerie blood mixed with the human blood.

And then I know what we have to do.
What I have to do.

19

Lucy

In the throne room, Soli turns around and sees me.
"You're awake!" she says. "Come sit down. We'll fill you
in."

I join them at the table, and Caro passes me a cup of
hot tea and a plate of cookies. I suddenly realize that I'm
starving.

"Thank you," I say, before cramming a cookie into my
mouth.

"We have a plan," Soli tells me.

"But you're not going to like it," Caro adds. When

Kheelan and Soli glare at her, she says, "What? She's not going to."

"You have to go back to the Crows," Soli explains.

I stop chewing and stare at them. "What? Why?" I ask.

"Because you're the only one who's safe to go," Kheelan says. "I'll bring you there tomorrow."

"What am I doing there?" I ask.

"You are convincing them to rejoin our kingdoms," Soli says.

"There's no way they'll agree to that," I say. "You weren't here when the leaders all talked. It was hard enough for Jonn to convince the peaceful leaders."

"Maybe you're right," Soli says. "It will be hard to convince any of them to join without Motherbird."

"Why would my mother agree to that?" I ask. "She wants to be queen of the Crows, remember? She doesn't care if the kingdoms are reunited.

Soli and Kheelan look at each other.

"We will make a deal with her," Soli says.

A shiver runs down my spine.

"What kind of deal?" I ask.

"A trade," Soli says. "If they join with us, we'll give them what they want."

"What do you mean?" I ask, but I already know.

"The blood of a halfling," Soli says. She holds out her wrist.

I want to cry, but I don't. And then I remember something. "What about the necklace?" I say. "She needs a necklace, too, and you can't reunite the kingdoms without a necklace."

Soli smiles. "It turns out that once the kingdoms reunite, the necklaces still exist. Or they turn into one necklace or something. But there's always a necklace. So we'll give her that."

"No, you won't," comes another voice.

We all turn.

A woman dressed in red stands in the entrance to the throne room.

Soli stands. "You must be Elsain," she says. "Welcome to Roseland."

The woman bows. "Thank you, Soledad," she says. "I wish I were here under happier circumstances."

"What do you mean about the necklace?" Caro asks. "Why won't it work? They agree to unite the kingdoms, and we give them the necklace once that's done."

"Because the necklace is the heartsource of the faerieground," Elsain explains calmly. "If it is destroyed, we are all destroyed. That's part of why we were split to begin with, millennia ago. Because it was too dangerous to be joined."

"But it's too dangerous not to be joined," Soli says. "Don't you agree?"

Elsain gazes at her and then nods. "I do agree," she says finally. "But we will have to find a different way. We cannot destroy the necklace."

"How else can we make Andria a faerie?" Soli asks. "That's what it will take."

Elsain is quiet for a while. Then she says, "I believe there is a way to rejoin the kingdoms in peace."

"What is it?" I ask, impatient. "And can we do it without using Soli's blood?"

Elsain sighs. "Georg has to die."

Soli

Of course Elsain is right.

Of course we have to kill Georg.

Then Caro will become queen, and she will agree to reunite the kingdoms, and we'll all live happily ever after in a beautiful, peaceful faerieground.

We all look at each other in the throne room.

"I can't kill my father," Caro says finally. "I hate him, he's terrible, but I can't kill him."

"You don't have to be the one to do it," Kheelan says.

Across the table, tears fall down Lucy's face.

"I don't want to be there when it happens," Caro says.

"You don't have to be," Kheelan says.

Elsain turns to go.

"Wait," I say. "Do you know what will happen? Don't all Ladybirds know the future?"

She smiles at me. "I do," she says. "I cannot tell you what will happen, but I can tell you that you will be brave." She looks at my friends. "You all will be brave."

Then she leaves.

We sit in silence in the throne room for a while longer. Then Caro stands.

"I can't be here while you make the plan," she says. "And you need to start to make the plan now. We're running out of time."

She leaves, and Kheelan and Lucy and I stare at each other across the table.

"I don't want to kill anyone," Lucy says.

"I don't either," I say. "If I do, how am I any better than Georg?"

Kheelan nods. "That's why I'm the one who has to do it," he says.

"I hate that idea," I say.

He gazes into my eyes. "I'm the only one who can, Soli."

Maybe he's right.

Maybe he was born to kill the Crow king.

But I don't know if I can love a murderer.

"It's the right thing to do, for the kingdom," he whispers. "It's the only thing to do. You have to let me do this for Roseland."

"We could just wait until Georg dies of old age," I say. "We can protect Roseland until then, can't we?"

Lucy snorts. "Against those people? No way," she says. "They're vicious."

"Not all of them," I say, thinking of Caro.

But then again, Caro is really only half-Crow.

"Georg might not die for hundreds of years," Kheelan says. "It isn't like your—"

He stops. Takes a breath.

"It isn't like the human world," he finishes. "We can't wait for him to die."

"Elsain told us what we have to do," I say finally.

Kheelan nods. "Leave it to me," he says. "There will be no blood on either of your hands."

I look at his strong, gentle hands.

How could I love a killer?

"Have you killed anyone before?" I ask. "I mean, not in battle."

He shakes his head. "No. I never thought I would," he says. "But I have to. For Roseland."

He stands. "I'll leave now. Tell Caro to be ready. She'll know when the king is gone."

20

Lucy

Kheelan leaves at nightfall, and Soli and Caro and I wait in the queen's quarters.

We don't talk. Soli reads from a book. Caro sharpens a knife against a long gray stone. I just wait.

I think about my mother, about to lose another husband.

It's strange to me that my mother loved someone besides my father. She always told me that she loved my dad more than she had ever loved anyone, besides me. When my dad died, she was devastated.

We both were.

I glance at Caro. I know how it feels to lose a father, but I don't know how it feels to lose a father like hers.

I always knew my dad loved me. Caro has been fighting for her father's love her whole life. That's why she is the way she is. That's why she's Caro the Betrayer.

Sitting here now, I guess, while someone goes to kill her father, is the ultimate betrayal.

Then I narrow my eyes, watching her.

Maybe she's tricking us. Maybe she's going to warn King Georg. Maybe she already has.

Soli

Hours after Kheelan rode toward the Crows, I look up from Andria's journal.

"Caro," I say. "You never read this?"

She shakes her head.

"Where did you find it?" I ask.

"In the greenhouse room," she tells me. "Why?"

I look down at Andria's handwriting again, swimming on the page in front of me.

"I think we were wrong," I say. "About Andria. But not about Georg."

I read out loud:

Calandra came to me in the night. She told me what she found.

A key to a secret passage, and a room full of evil. Descriptions of my every move. Dark spells. War plans.

I didn't believe her, so she showed me.

Georg wants to take over the faerieground. He's a murderer. He and his Crows have killed thousands already. They stop at nothing.

He wasn't lying about turning me into a faerie. There's a spell. It's all written in the books.

To make me full faerie, he needs the blood of a halfling.

The only halfling here is Caro. My daughter.

I will leave tonight. I can't take Caro with me. I don't know the spells to protect a faerie in the human world.

Calandra will need to stay behind so that he doesn't come after me, but she will come home soon.

I don't think he'll care that I'm gone. He'll just care that the beloved Crow queen is gone. He'll be embarrassed. He won't miss me.

I feel like a fool for not knowing he never loved me.

Calandra came to me in the night. She told me what she found.

A Key to a secret ~~gate~~ passage, and a room full of evil.

Descriptions of my every move. Dark spells. WAR PLANS.

I didn't believe her, so she showed me.

Georg wants to take over the faerieground. He's a murderer.

He and his Crows have killed thousands already.

They stop at nothing

He wasn't lying about ~~me~~ turning me into a faerie.

There's a spell. It's all written in the books. To make me full fae he needs the blood of a halfling. The only halfling here is Caro.

My Daughter.

I will leave tonight. I can't take Caro with me. I don't know the spells to protect a faerie in the human world.

Calandiva will need to stay behind, so that he doesn't come after me. but she will come home soon.

I don't think he'll care that I'm gone. He'll just care that the beloved Crow Queen is gone.

He'll be embarrassed. He won't miss me.

I feel like a fool for not knowing he never loved me.

That's the last page in the book.

Lucy and Caro stare at me. "So she's not back to help take over the faerieground?" Caro says finally.

"I think she came back for you," I admit. "And Lucy, of course."

"At least this means we know Kheelan is doing the right thing," Lucy says. "Georg needs to be stopped."

Caro shivers. Then she looks at me.

"I think he's gone," she says.

"Did you feel it?" I ask. "Can you tell?"

She nods, and one tear slips from her eye.

We are quiet for a while.

After an hour or two, Jonn comes into my rooms, a solemn look on his face.

"We have just received a message from the Crows," he says.

"We know," I say, glancing at Caro. "Georg is gone."

Jonn nods.

"Is Kheelan okay?" I ask.

He looks confused. "Why do you ask that?" he says. "Why wouldn't he be?"

Caro and Lucy and I look at each other. "Because he went to kill Georg," I say slowly. "He didn't tell you?"

Jonn shakes his head. "He didn't kill Georg," he says. "Andria did."

She came back to stop Georg and save her daughters. And to save me.

Even the Ladybirds were wrong about Andria.

When we find her, hours later, traveling toward Roseland in the forest outside the Crow palace, she is crying and exhausted.

She hugs Lucy first, and then she stares at Caro.

"Is it you?" Andria whispers. "Caro?"

Caro smiles. "Hello, again," she says. "I've missed you."

They hug, and Andria steps back to look at both of her daughters.

"We thought you were here to destroy the faerieground," I say. "I'm so sorry I didn't know."

Andria smiles. "How could you have known?" she asks. "The only person who knew was Calandra. I promised her."

Then she turns to Caro. "You're the queen now," she says. "Do what you know is right."

Caro nods, and Lucy smiles. "I forgot!" Lucy says. "Here's your necklace."

She takes the blue pendant and slips it over Caro's head.

And I can see the queen inside Caro, who no longer is a betrayer.

* * *

After we walk back to Roseland, after the other kings and queens are gathered, after the kingdoms have been restored to one glorious faerieground, after Andria goes home with Lucy, and after some years have passed, Kheelan and I will marry.

We will have a daughter, and I will name her Lucy.

I will tell her stories about my childhood, but we will not cross back over to the human world.

We will seal the borders, so that the worlds are separate, so that no magic can slip through the walls.

But even when I'm a thousand years old, I will never forget Lucy, my almost-sister, my best friend.

The sun to my shadow.

The girl who believed in me.

Andria

When I left the faerieground the first time, I hoped I'd never have to return. But when Lucy was taken—when Lucy came home with the Equinox pendant—I knew I'd have to. Georg was still out there, and he had to be stopped.

I was the only one who could stop him.

He had a plan, a plan to take over all of the faerieground.

When I came back, we'd destroy the necklace and murder the halfling. With the necklace destroyed, the kingdoms couldn't be united. But they could be won.

He's the one who stole the Roseland necklace for me. He's the one who, later, tricked the Ladybirds into giving me Soli. He thought we were ready. But I was never going to do those things.

I loved my sister, and I loved her daughter. And I loved my daughters—the one I thought I'd never see again, but who I hoped would be protected. And the one who lived with me, who I hoped would never walk into the woods.

When I came back to the faerieground I had to pretend as if everything was normal, as if the plan was in effect. I had to screw up my courage and kiss that monster. We had to laugh together and talk about how finally, finally, our time had come.

And then, when the sun had set over the Equinox kingdom, and the children had been given time to get away, I had to kill him. I had to slit his throat with his own sword.

It was the only way.

I am not a murderer, but I could not let him live in this world. Even if this world is not my own, I have always loved it.

21

Lucy

At bedtime, Lina asks for faerie stories. I tell her tales about Queen Soledad and her husband, King Kheelan. I tell her about Queen Carolin. I tell her how the seven kingdoms of the faerieground were ripped apart and then sewn carefully back together, stitched by fourteen hands.

I tell her about the woods. How they are very like the woods near our own house, except that the air is clearer, the animals are unfamiliar, the trees are taller and their leaves greener. I tell her how the woods go on forever.

I tell her how the food there is made of wildflowers and sweet leaves, how clothes are woven out of the fluff from dandelions, how there are metals more precious than gold and gems clearer than diamonds.

And I tell her how if she makes a wish in the woods near our house, the faeries might let her slip over to their side. How they used to be cruel, some of them, but now they're kind.

She snuggles close to me, says she doesn't want to visit the faerieground. Maybe when she's older, she tells me.

Yes, I think. *Maybe I'll go back, too.*

And every night, she asks if I believe in faeries. She asks if the stories are true.

"I don't know," I tell her.

For all I know, they could be.

Beth & Kay

Kay Fraser and *Beth Bracken* are a designer-editor team in Minnesota.

Kay is from Buenos Aires. She left home at eighteen and moved to North Dakota—basically the exact opposite of Argentina. These days, she designs books, writes, makes tea for her husband, and drives their daughters to their dance lessons.

Beth lives in a light-filled house in Minneapolis with her husband and their children, Sam and Etta. Beth spends her time editing books, reading, daydreaming, and rearranging her furniture.

Kay and Beth both love dark chocolate, Buffy, and tea.

Odessa

Odessa Sawyer is an illustrator from Santa Fe, New Mexico. She works mainly in digital mixed media, utilizing digital painting, photography, and traditional pen and ink.

Odessa's work has graced the book covers of many top publishing houses, and she has also done work for various film and television projects, posters, and album covers.

Highly influenced by fantasy, fairy tales, fashion, and classic horror, Odessa's work celebrates a whimsical, dreamy, and vibrant quality.

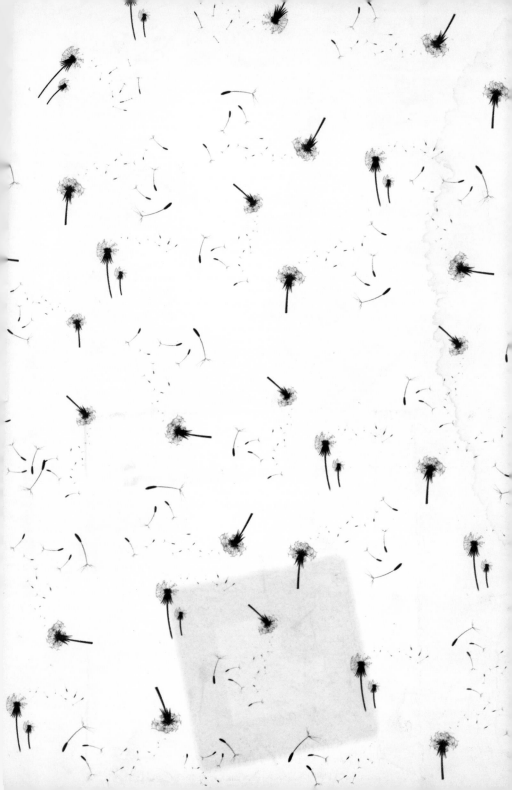